AN EYE FOR AN EYE

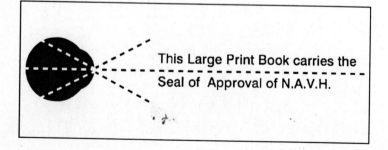

AN EYE FOR AN EYE

ANTHONY TROLLOPE

KENNEBEC LARGE PRINT
A part of Gale, Cengage Learning

GALE
CENGAGE Learning·

Detroit • New York • San Francisco • New Haven, Conn • Waterville, Maine • London

GALE
CENGAGE Learning™

Kennebec Large Print, a part of Gale, Cengage Learning.
Kennebec Large Print® Perennial Favorites Collection.
The text of this Large Print edition is unabridged.
Other aspects of the book may vary from the original edition.
Set in 16 pt. Plantin.

LIBRARY OF CONGRESS CATALOGING-IN-PUBLICATION DATA

Trollope, Anthony, 1815–1882.
  An eye for an eye / by Anthony Trollope.
    p. cm. — (Kennebec Large Print perennial favorites collection)
  ISBN-13: 978-1-4104-3583-5 (pbk.)
  ISBN-10: 1-4104-3583-0 (pbk.)
  1. Man-woman relationships—Fiction. 2. Mothers and daughters—Fiction. 3. Revenge—Fiction. 4. Ireland—Fiction. 5. Domestic fiction. 6. Large
type books. I. Title.
  PR5684.E9 2011
  823'.8—dc22   2010049760

Originally published in 1879 and is now in Public Domain in the United States.

Printed in the United States of America
  1 2 3 4 5   15 14 13 12 11

ED042

CONTENTS

■ ■ ■ ■

VOLUME I.

■ ■ ■ ■

INTRODUCTION.

At a private asylum in the west of England there lives, and has lived for some years past, an unfortunate lady, as to whom there has long since ceased to be any hope that she should ever live elsewhere. Indeed, there is no one left belonging to her by whom the indulgence of such a hope on her behalf could be cherished. Friends she has none; and her own condition is such, that she recks nothing of confinement and does not even sigh for release. And yet her mind is ever at work, — as is doubtless always the case with the insane. She has present to her, apparently in every waking moment of her existence, an object of intense interest, and at that she works with a constancy which never wearies herself, however fatiguing it may be to those who are near her. She is ever justifying some past action of her life. "An eye for an eye," she says, "and a tooth for a tooth. Is it not the law?" And these words she will repeat daily, almost from morn till night.

It has been said that this poor lady has no friends. Friends who would be anxious for her recovery, who would care to see her even in her wretched condition, who might try to soothe her harassed heart with words of love, she has none. Such is her condition now, and her temperament, that it may be doubted whether any words of love, however tender, could be efficacious with her. She is always demanding justification, and as those who are around her never thwart her she has probably all the solace which kindness could give her.

But, though she has no friends — none who love her, — she has all the material comfort which friendship or even love could supply. All that money can do to lessen her misery, is done. The house in which she lives is surrounded by soft lawns and secluded groves. It has been prepared altogether for the wealthy, and is furnished with every luxury which it may be within the power of a maniac to enjoy. This lady has her own woman to attend her; and the woman, though stout and masterful, is gentle in language and kind in treatment. "An eye for an eye, ma'am. Oh, certainly. That is the law. An eye for an eye, no doubt." This formula she will repeat a dozen times a day — ay, a dozen dozen times, till the wonder is that she also should not be mad.

The reader need not fear that he is to be asked to loiter within the precincts of an asylum for the insane. Of this abode of wretchedness no word more shall be said; but the story shall be told of the lady who dwelt there, — the story of her life till madness placed her within those walls. That story was known to none at the establishment but to him who was its head. Others there, who were cognisant of the condition of the various patients, only knew that from quarter to quarter the charges for this poor lady's custody were defrayed by the Earl of Scroope.

CHAPTER I.
SCROOPE MANOR.

Some years ago, it matters not how many, the old Earl of Scroope lived at Scroope Manor in Dorsetshire. The house was an Elizabethan structure of some pretensions, but of no fame. It was not known to sight-seers, as are so many of the residences of our nobility and country gentlemen. No days in the week were appointed for visiting its glories, nor was the housekeeper supposed to have a good thing in perquisites from showing it. It was a large brick building facing on to the village street, — facing the village, if the hall-door of a house be the main characteristic of its face; but with a front on to its own grounds from which opened the windows of the chief apartments. The village of Scroope consisted of a straggling street a mile in length, with the church and parsonage at one end, and the Manor-house almost at the other. But the church stood within the park; and on that side of the street, for more than half its length, the high, gloomy wall of the Earl's domain stretched along in face of the publicans, bakers, grocers, two butchers, and retired private residents whose almost contiguous houses made Scroope itself seem to be more than a village to strangers. Close to the Manor and again near to the church, some favoured few had been allowed to build houses and to cultivate small gardens taken, as it were, in notches out of the Manor grounds; but these tenements must have been built at a time in which landowners were very much less jealous than they are now of such encroachments from their humbler neighbours.

The park itself was large, and the appendages to it such as were fit for an Earl's establishment; — but there was little about it that was attractive. The land lay flat, and the timber, which was very plentiful, had not been made to group itself in picturesque forms. There was the Manor wood, containing some five hundred acres, lying beyond the church and far back from the road, intersected with so-called drives, which were unfit for any wheels but those of timber waggons; — and round the whole park there was a broad belt of trees. Here and there about the large enclosed spaces there stood solitary oaks, in which the old Earl took pride; but at Scroope Manor there was none of that finished landscape beauty of which the owners of "places" in England are so justly proud.

The house was large, and the rooms were grand and spacious. There was an enormous hall into one corner of which the front door opened. There was a vast library filled with old books which no one ever touched, — huge volumes of antiquated and now all but useless theology, and folio editions of the least known classics, — such as men now never read. Not a book had been added to it since the commencement of the century, and it may almost be said that no book had been drawn from its shelves for real use during the same period. There was a suite of rooms, — a salon with two withdrawing rooms which now were never opened. The big dining-room was used occasionally, as, in accordance with the traditions of the family, dinner was served there whenever there were guests at the Manor. Guests, indeed, at Scroope Manor were not very frequent; — but Lady Scroope did occasionally have a friend or two to stay with her; and at long intervals the country clergymen and neighbouring squires were asked, with their wives, to dinner. When the Earl and his Countess were alone they used a small breakfast parlour, and between this and the big dining-room there was the little chamber in which the Countess usually lived. The Earl's own room was at the back, or if the reader pleases, front of the house, near the door leading into the street, and was, of all rooms in the house, the gloomiest.

The atmosphere of the whole place was gloomy. There were none of those charms of modern creation which now make the mansions of the wealthy among us bright and joyous. There was not a billiard table in the house. There was no conservatory nearer than the large old-fashioned greenhouse, which stood away by the kitchen garden and which seemed to belong exclusively to the gardener. The papers on the walls were dark and sombre. The mirrors were small and lustreless. The carpets were old and dingy. The windows did not open on to the terrace. The furniture was hardly ancient, but yet antiquated and uncomfortable. Throughout the house, and indeed throughout the estate, there was sufficient evidence of wealth; and there certainly was no evidence of parsimony; but at Scroope Manor money seemed never to have produced luxury. The household was very large. There was a butler, and a housekeeper, and various footmen, and a cook with large wages, and maidens in tribes to wait upon each other, and a colony of gardeners, and a coachman, and a head-groom, and under-grooms. All these lived well under the old Earl, and knew the value of their privileges. There was much to get, and almost nothing to do. A servant might live for ever at Scroope Manor, — if only sufficiently submissive to Mrs. Bunce the housekeeper. There was certainly no parsimony at the Manor, but the luxurious living of the household was confined to the servants' department.

To a stranger, and perhaps also to the inmates, the idea of gloom about the place was greatly increased by the absence of any garden or lawn near the house. Immediately in front of the mansion, and between it and the park, there ran two broad gravel terraces, one above another; and below these the deer would come and browse.

To the left of the house, at nearly a quarter of a mile distant from it, there was a very large garden indeed, — flower-gardens, and kitchen-gardens, and orchards; all ugly, and old-fashioned, but producing excellent crops in their kind. But they were away, and were not seen. Oat flowers were occasionally brought into the house, — but the place was never filled with flowers as country houses are filled with them now-a-days. No doubt had Lady Scroope wished for more she might have had more.

Scroope itself, though a large village, stood a good deal out of the world. Within the last year or two a railway has been opened, with a Scroope Road Station, not above three miles from the place; but in the old lord's time it was eleven miles from its nearest station, at Dorchester, with which it had communication once a day by an omnibus. Unless a man had business with Scroope nothing would take him there; and very few people had business with Scroope. Now and then a commercial traveller would visit the place with but faint hopes as to trade. A post-office inspector once in twelve months would call upon plethoric old Mrs. Applejohn, who kept the small shop for stationery, and was known as the postmistress. The two sons of the vicar, Mr. Greenmarsh, would pass backwards and forwards between their father's vicarage and Marl-bro' school. And occasionally the men and women of Scroope would make a journey to their county town. But the Earl was told that old

16

Mrs. Brock of the Scroope Arms could not keep the omnibus on the road unless he would subscribe to aid it. Of course he subscribed. If he had been told by his steward to subscribe to keep the cap on Mrs. Brock's head, he would have done so. Twelve pounds a year his Lordship paid towards the omnibus, and Scroope was not absolutely dissevered from the world.

The Earl himself was never seen out of his own domain, except when he attended church. This he did twice every Sunday in the year, the coachman driving him there in the morning and the head-groom in the afternoon. Throughout the household it was known to be the Earl's request to his servants that they would attend divine service at least once every Sunday. None were taken into service but they who were or who called themselves members of the Church Establishment. It is hardly probable that many dissenters threw away the chance of such promotion on any frivolous pretext of religion. Beyond this request, which, coming from the mouth of Mrs. Bunce, became very imperative, the Earl hardly ever interfered with his domestics. His own valet had attended him for the last thirty years; but, beyond his valet and the butler, he hardly knew the face of one of them. There was a gamekeeper at Scroope Manor, with two under-gamekeepers; and yet, for, some years, no one, except the gamekeepers, had ever shot over the lands. Some partridges and a few pheasants were, however, sent into the house when Mrs.

17

Bunce, moved to wrath, would speak her mind on that subject.

The Earl of Scroope himself was a tall, thin man, something over seventy at the time of which I will now begin to speak. His shoulders were much bent, but otherwise he appeared to be younger than his age. His hair was nearly white, but his eyes were still bright, and the handsome well-cut features of his fine face were not reduced to shapelessness by any of the ravages of time, as is so often the case with men who are infirm as well as old. Were it not for the long and heavy eyebrows, which gave something of severity to his face, and for that painful stoop in his shoulders, he might still have been accounted a handsome man. In youth he had been a very handsome man, and had shone forth in the world, popular, beloved, respected, with all the good things the world could give. The first blow upon him was the death of his wife. That hurt him sorely, but it did not quite crush him. Then his only daughter died also, just as she became a bride. High as the Lady Blanche Neville had stood herself, she had married almost above her rank, and her father's heart had been full of joy and pride. But she had perished childless, — in child-birth, and again he was hurt almost to death. There was still left to him a son, — a youth indeed thoughtless, lavish, and prone to evil pleasures. But thought would come with years; for almost any lavishness there were means sufficient; and evil

18

pleasures might cease to entice. The young Lord Neville was all that was left to the Earl, and for his heir he paid debts and forgave injuries. The young man would marry and all might be well. Then he found a bride for his boy, — with no wealth, but owning the best blood in the kingdom, beautiful, good, one who might be to him as another daughter. His boy's answer was that he was already married! He had chosen his wife from out of the streets, and offered to the Earl of Scroope as a child to replace the daughter who had gone, a wretched painted prostitute from France. After that Lord Scroope never again held up his head.

The father would not see his heir, — and never saw him again. As to what money might be needed, the lawyers in London were told to manage that. The Earl himself would give nothing and refuse nothing. When there were debts, — debts for the second time, debts for the third time, the lawyers were instructed to do what in their own eyes seemed good to them. They might pay as long as they deemed it right to pay, but they might not name Lord Neville to his father.

While things were thus the Earl married again, — the penniless daughter of a noble house, — a woman not young, for she was forty when he married her, but more than twenty years his junior. It sufficed for him that she was noble, and as he believed good. Good to him she was, — with a duty that was almost excessive. Religious she was, and self-denying; giving much

19

and demanding little; keeping herself in the background, but possessing wonderful energy in the service of others. Whether she could in truth be called good the reader may say when he has finished this story.

Then, when the Earl had been married some three years to his second wife, the heir died. He died, and as far as Scroope Manor was concerned there was an end of him and of the creature he had called his wife. An annuity was purchased for her. That she should be entitled to call herself Lady Neville while she lived, was the sad necessity of the condition. It was understood by all who came near the Earl that no one was to mention her within his hearing. He was thankful that no heir had come from that most horrid union. The woman was never mentioned to him again, nor need she trouble us further in the telling of our chronicle.

But when Lord Neville died, it was necessary that the old man should think of his new heir. Alas; in that family, though there was much that was good and noble, there had ever been intestine feuds, — causes of quarrel in which each party would be sure that he was right. They were a people who thought much of the church, who were good to the poor, who strove to be noble; — but they could not forgive injuries. They could not forgive even when there were no injuries. The present Earl had quarrelled with his brother in early life; — and had therefore quarrelled with all that had belonged to the brother. The brother was now gone, leaving two sons behind him, — two young Nevilles, Fred and Jack, of whom Fred, the eldest, was now the heir. It was at last settled that Fred should be sent for to Scroope Manor. Fred came, being at that time a lieutenant in a cavalry regiment, — a fine handsome youth of five and twenty, with the Neville eyes and Neville finely cut features. Kindly letters passed between the widowed mother and the present Lady Scroope; and it was decided at last, at his own request, that he should remain one year longer in the army, and then be installed as the eldest son at Scroope Manor. Again the lawyer was told to do what was proper in regard to money.

A few words more must be said of Lady Scroope, and then the preface to our story will be over. She too was an Earl's daughter, and had been much loved by our Earl's first wife. Lady Scroope had been the elder by ten years; but yet they had been dear friends, and Lady Mary Wycombe had passed many months of her early life amidst the gloom of the great rooms at Scroope Manor. She had thus known the Earl well before she consented to marry him. She had never possessed beauty, — and hardly grace. She was strong featured, tall, with pride clearly written in her face. A reader of faces would have declared at once that she was proud of the blood which ran in her veins. She was very proud of her blood, and did in truth believe that noble birth was a greater gift than any wealth. She was thoroughly able to look down upon a parvenu millionaire, — to look down upon such a one and not to pretend to despise him. When the Earl's letter came to her asking her to share his gloom, she was as poor as Charity, — dependent on a poor brother who hated the burden of such claim. But she would have wedded no commoner, let his wealth and age have been as they might. She knew Lord Scroope's age, and she knew the gloom of Scroope Manor; — and she became his wife. To her of course was told the story of the heir's marriage, and she knew that she could expect no light, no joy in the old house from the scions of the rising family. But now all this was changed, and it might be that she could take the new heir to her heart.

Chapter II.
Fred Neville.

When Fred Neville first came to the Manor, the old Earl trembled when called upon to receive him. Of the lad he had heard almost nothing, — of his appearance literally nothing. It might be that his heir would be meanly visaged, a youth of whom he would have cause to be ashamed, one from whose countenance no sign of high blood would shine out; or, almost worse, he also might have that look, half of vanity, and half of vice, of which the father had gradually become aware in his own son, and which in him had degraded the Neville beauty. But Fred, to look at, was a gallant fellow, — such a youth as women love to see about a house, — well-made, active, quick, self-asserting, fair-haired, blue-eyed, short-lipped, with small whiskers, thinking but little of his own personal advantages, but thinking much of his own way. As far as the appearance of the young man went the Earl could not but be satisfied. And to him, at any rate in this, the beginning of their connexion, Fred Neville was modest and submissive. "You are welcome to Scroope," said the old man, receiving him with stately urbanity in the middle of the hall. "I am so much obliged to you, uncle," he said. "You are come to me as a son, my boy, — as a son. It will be your own fault if you are not a son to us in everything." Then in lieu of further words there shone a tear in each of the young man's eyes, much more eloquent to the Earl than could have been any words. He put his arm over his nephew's shoulders, and in this guise walked with him into the room in which Lady Scroope was awaiting them. "Mary," he said to his wife, "here is our heir. Let him be a son to us." Then Lady Scroope took the young man in her arms and kissed him. Thus auspiciously was commenced this new connexion.

The arrival was in September, and the gamekeeper, with the under gamekeeper, had for the last month been told to be on his mettle. Young Mr. Neville was no doubt a sportsman. And the old groom had been warned that hunters might be wanted in the stables next winter. Mrs. Bunce was made to understand that liberties would probably be taken with the house, such as had not yet been perpetrated in her time; — for the late heir had never made the Manor his home from the time of his leaving school. It was felt by all that great changes were to be effected, — and it was felt also that the young man on whose behalf all this was to be permitted, could not but be elated by his position. Of such elation, however, there were not many signs. To his uncle, Fred Neville was, as has been said, modest and submissive; to his aunt he was gentle but not submissive. The rest of the household he treated civilly, but with none of that awe which was perhaps expected from him. As for shooting, he had come direct from his friend Carnaby's moor. Carnaby had forest as well as moor, and Fred thought but little of partridges, — little of such old-fashioned partridge-shooting as was prepared for him at Scroope, — after grouse and deer. As for hunting in Dorsetshire, if his uncle wished it, — why in that case he would think of it. According to his ideas, Dorsetshire was not the best county in England for hunting. Last year his regiment had been at Bristol and he had ridden with the Duke's hounds. This winter he was to be stationed in Ireland, and he had an idea that Irish hunting was good. If he found that his uncle made a point of it, he would bring his horses to Scroope for a month at Christmas. Thus he spoke to the head groom, — and thus he spoke also to his aunt, who felt some surprise when he talked of Scotland and his horses. She had thought that only men of large fortunes shot deer and kept studs, — and perhaps conceived that the officers of the 20th Hussars were generally engaged in looking after the affairs of their regiment, and in preparation for meeting the enemy.

Fred now remained a month at Scroope, and during that time there was but little personal intercourse between him and his uncle in spite of the affectionate greeting with which their acquaintance had been commenced. The old man's habits of life were so confirmed that he could not bring himself to alter them. Throughout the entire morning he would sit in his own room alone. He would then be visited by his steward, his groom, and his butler; — and would think that he gave his orders, submitting, however, in almost every thing to them. His wife would sometimes sit with him for half an hour, holding his hand, in moments of tenderness unseen and unsuspected by all the world around them. Sometimes the clergyman of the parish would come to him, so that he might know the wants of the people. He would have the newspaper in his hands for a while, and would daily read the Bible for an hour. Then he would slowly write some letter, almost measuring every point which his pen made, — thinking that thus he was performing his duty as a man of business. Few men perhaps did less, — but what he did do was good; and of self-indulgence there was surely none. Between such a one and the young man who had now come to his house there could be but little real connexion.

Between Fred Neville and Lady Scroope there arose a much closer intimacy. A woman can get nearer to a young man than can any old man; — can learn more of his ways, and better understand his wishes. From the very first there arose between them a matter of difference, as to which there was no quarrel, but very much of argument. In that argument Lady Scroope was unable to prevail. She was very anxious that the heir should at once abandon his profession and sell out of the army. Of what use could it be to him now to run after his regiment to Ireland, seeing that undoubtedly the great duties of his life all centred at Scroope? There were many discussions on the subject, but Fred would not give way in regard to the next year. He would have this year, he said, to himself; — and after that he would come and settle himself at Scroope. Yes; no doubt he would marry as soon as he could find a fitting wife. Of course it would be right that he should marry. He fully understood the responsibilities of his position; — so he said, in answer to his aunt's eager, scrutinising, beseeching questions. But as he had joined his regiment, he thought it would be good for him to remain with it one year longer. He particularly desired to see something of Ireland, and if he did not do so now, he would never have the opportunity. Lady Scroope, understanding well that he was pleading for a year of grace from the dulness of the Manor, explained to him that his uncle would by no means expect that he should remain always at Scroope. If he would marry, the old London house should be prepared for him and his bride. He might travel, — not, however, going very far afield. He might get into Parliament; as to which, if such were his ambition, his uncle would give him every aid. He might have his friends at Scroope Manor, — Carnaby and all the rest of them. Every allurement was offered to him. But he had commenced by claiming a year of grace, and to that claim he adhered.

Could his uncle have brought himself to make the request in person, at first, he might probably have succeeded; — and had he succeeded, there would have been no story for us as to the fortunes of Scroope Manor. But the Earl was too proud and perhaps too diffident to make the attempt. From his wife he heard all that took place; and though he was grieved, he expressed no anger. He could not feel himself justified in expressing anger because his nephew chose to remain for yet a year attached to his profession. "Who knows what may happen to him?" said the Countess.

"Ah, indeed! But we are all in the hands of the Almighty." And the Earl bowed his head. Lady Scroope, fully recognizing the truth of her husband's pious ejaculation, nevertheless thought that human care might advantageously be added to the divine interposition for which, as she well knew, her lord prayed fervently as soon as the words were out of his mouth.

"But it would be so great a thing if he could be settled. Sophia Mellerby has promised to come here for a couple of months in the winter. He could not possibly do better than that."

"The Mellerbys are very good people," said the Earl. "Her grandmother, the duchess, is one of the very best women in England. Her mother, Lady Sophia, is an excellent creature, — religious, and with the soundest principles. Mr. Mellerby, as a commoner, stands as high as any man in England."

"They have held the same property since the wars of the roses. And then I suppose the money should count for something," added the lady.

Lord Scroope would not admit the importance of the money, but was quite willing to acknowledge that were his heir to make Sophia Mellerby the future Lady Scroope he would be content. But he could not interfere. He did not think it wise to speak to young men on such a subject. He thought that by doing so a young man might be rather diverted from than attracted to the object in view. Nor would he press his wishes upon his nephew as to next year. "Were I to ask it," he said, "and were he to refuse me, I should be hurt. I am bound therefore to ask nothing that is unreasonable." Lady Scroope did not quite agree with her husband in this. She thought that as every thing was to be done for the young man; as money almost without stint was to be placed at his command; as hunting, parliament, and a house in London were offered to him; — as the treatment due to a dear and only son was shown to him, he ought to give something in return; but she herself, could say no more than she had said, and she knew already that in those few matters in which her husband had a decided will, he was not to be turned from it.

It was arranged, therefore, that Fred Neville

should join his regiment at Limerick in October, and that he should come home to Scroope for a fortnight or three weeks at Christmas. Sophia Mellerby was to be Lady Scroope's guest at that time, and at last it was decided that Mrs. Neville, who had never been seen by the Earl, should be asked to come and bring with her her younger son, John Neville, who had been successful in obtaining a commission in the Engineers. Other guests should be invited, and an attempt should be made to remove the mantle of gloom from Scroope Manor, — with the sole object of ingratiating the heir.

Early in October Fred went to Limerick, and from thence with a detached troop of his regiment he was sent to the cavalry barracks at Ennis, the assize town of the neighbouring County Clare. This was at first held to be a misfortune by him, as Limerick is in all respects a better town than Ennis, and in County Limerick the hunting is far from being bad, whereas Clare is hardly a country for a Nimrod. But a young man, with money at command, need not regard distances; and the Limerick balls and the Limerick coverts were found to be equally within reach. From Ennis also he could attend some of the Galway meets, — and then with no other superior than a captain hardly older than himself to interfere with his movements, he could indulge in that wild district the spirit of adventure which was strong within him. When young men are anxious to indulge the spirit of adventure, they generally do so by falling in love with young women of whom their fathers and mothers would not approve. In these days a spirit of adventure hardly goes further than this, unless it take a young man to a German gambling table.

When Fred left Scroope it was understood that he was to correspond with his aunt. The Earl would have been utterly lost had he attempted to write a letter to his nephew without having something special to communicate to him. But Lady Scroope was more facile with her pen, and it was rightly thought that the heir would hardly bring himself to look upon Scroope as his home, unless some link were maintained between himself and the place. Lady Scroope therefore wrote once a week, — telling everything that there was to be told of the horses, the game, and even of the tenants. She studied her letters, endeavouring to make them light and agreeable, — such as a young man of large prospects would like to receive from his own mother. He was "Dearest Fred," and in one of those earliest written she expressed a hope that should any trouble ever fall upon him he would come to her as to his dearest friend. Fred was not a bad correspondent, and answered about every other letter. His replies were short, but that was a matter of course. He was "as jolly as a sandboy," "right as a trivet;" had had "one or two very good things," and thought that upon the whole he liked Ennis better than Limerick. "Johnstone is such a deuced good fellow!" Johnstone was the captain of the 20th Hussars who happened to be stationed with him at Limerick. Lady Scroope did not quite like the epithet, but she knew that she had to learn to hear things to which she had hitherto not been accustomed.

This was all very well; — but Lady Scroope, having a friend in Co. Clare, thought that she might receive tidings of the adopted one which would be useful, and with this object she opened a correspondence with Lady Mary Quin. Lady Mary Quin was a daughter of the Earl of Kilfenora, and was well acquainted with all County Clare. She was almost sure to hear of the doings of any officers stationed at Ennis, and would do so certainly in regard to an officer that was specially introduced to her. Fred Neville was invited to stay at Castle Quin as long as he pleased, and actually did pass one night under its roof. But, unfortunately for him, that spirit of adventure which he was determined to indulge led him into the neighbourhood of Castle Quin when it was far from his intention to interfere with the Earl or with Lady Mary, and thus led to the following letter which Lady Scroope received about the middle of December, — just a week before Fred's return to the Manor.

Quin Castle, Ennistimon,
14 December, 18—.
MY DEAR LADY SCROOPE,
     Since I wrote to you before, Mr. Neville has been here once, and we all liked him very

much. My father was quite taken with him. He is always fond of the young officers, and is not the less inclined to be so of one who is so dear and near to you. I wish he would have stayed longer, and hope that he shall come again. We have not much to offer in the way of amusement, but in January and February there is good snipe shooting.

I find that Mr. Neville is very fond of shooting, — so much so that before we knew anything of him except his name we had heard that he had been on our coast after seals and sea birds. We have very high cliffs near here, — some people say the highest in the world, and there is one called the Hag's Head from which men get down and shoot sea-gulls. He has been different times in our village of Liscannor, and I think he has a boat there or at Lahinch. I believe he has already killed ever so many seals.

I tell you all this for a reason. I hope that it may come to nothing, but I think that you ought to know. There is a widow lady living not very far from Liscannor, but nearer up to the cliffs. Her cottage is on papa's property, but I think she holds it from somebody else. I don't like to say anything to papa about it. Her name is Mrs. O'Hara, and she has a daughter.

When Lady Scroope had read so far, she almost let the paper drop from her hand. Of course she knew what it all meant. An Irish Miss O'Hara! And Fred Neville was spending his time in pursuit of this girl! Lady Scroope had known what it would be when the young man was allowed to return to his regiment in spite of the manifold duties which should have bound him to Scroope Manor.

I have seen this young lady,

continued Lady Mary,

and she is certainly very pretty. But nobody knows anything about them; and I cannot even learn whether they belong to the real O'Haras. I should think not, as they are Roman Catholics. At any rate Miss O'Hara can hardly be a fitting companion for Lord Scroope's heir. I believe they are ladies, but I don't think that any one knows them here, except the priest of Kilmacrenny. We never could make out quite why they came here, — only that Father Marty knows something about them. He is the priest of Kilmacrenny. She is a very pretty girl, and I never heard a word against her; — but I don't know whether that does not make it worse, because a young man is so likely to get entangled.

I daresay nothing shall come of it, and I'm sure I hope that nothing may. But I thought it best to tell you. Pray do not let him know that you have heard from me. Young men are so very particular about things, and I don't know what he might say of me if he knew that I had written home to you about his private affairs. All the same if I can be of any service to you, pray let me know. Excuse haste. And believe me to be,

Yours most sincerely,
MARY QUIN.

A Roman Catholic; — one whom no one knew but the priest; — a girl who perhaps never had a father! All this was terrible to Lady Scroope. Roman Catholics, — and especially Irish Roman Catholics, — were people whom, as she thought, every one should fear in this world, and for whom everything was to be feared in the next. How would it be with the Earl if this heir also were to tell him some day that he was married? Would not his grey hairs be brought to the grave with a double load of sorrow? However, for the present she thought it better to say not a word to the Earl.

CHAPTER III.
SOPHIE MELLERBY.

Lady Scroope thought a great deal about her friend's communication, but at last made up her mind that she could do nothing till Fred should have returned. Indeed she hardly knew what she could do when he did come back. The more she considered it the greater seemed to her to be the difficulty of doing anything. How is a woman, how is even a mother, to caution a young man against the danger of becoming acquainted with a pretty girl? She could not mention Miss O'Hara's name without mentioning that of Lady Mary Quin in connexion with it. And when asked, as of course she would be asked, as to her own information, what could she say? She had been told that he had made himself acquainted with a widow lady who had a pretty daughter, and that was all! When young men will run into such difficulties, it is, alas, so very difficult to interfere with them!

And yet the matter was of such importance as to justify almost any interference. A Roman Catholic Irish girl of whom nothing was known but that her mother was said to be a widow, was, in Lady Scroope's eyes, as formidable a danger as could come in the way of her husband's heir. Fred Neville was, she thought, with all his good qualities, exactly the man to fall in love with a wild Irish girl. If Fred were to write home some day and say that he was about to marry such a bride, — or, worse again, that he had married her, the tidings would nearly kill the Earl. After all that had been endured, such a termination to the hopes of the family would be too cruel! And Lady Scroope could not but feel the injustice of it. Every thing was being done for this heir, for whom nothing need have been done. He was treated as a son, but he was not a son. He was treated with exceptional favour as a son. Everything was at his disposal. He might marry and begin life at once with every want amply supplied, if he would only marry such a woman as was fit to be a future Countess of Scroope. Very little was required from him. He was not expected to marry an heiress. An heiress indeed was prepared for him, and would be there, ready for him at Christmas, — an heiress, beautiful, well-born, fit in every respect, — religious too. But he was not to be asked to marry Sophie Mellerby. He might choose for himself. There were other well-born young women about the world, — duchesses' granddaughters in abundance! But it was imperative that he should marry at least a lady, and at least a Protestant.

Lady Scroope felt very strongly that he should never have been allowed to rejoin his regiment, when a home at Scroope was offered to him. He was a free agent of course, and equally of course the title and the property must ultimately be his. But something of a bargain might have been made with him when all the privileges of a son were offered to him. When he was told that he might have all Scroope to himself, — for it amounted nearly to that; that he might hunt there and shoot there and entertain his friends; that the family house in London should be given up to him if he would marry properly; that an income almost without limit should be provided for him, surely it would not have been too much to demand that as a matter of course he should leave the army! But this had not been done; and now there was an Irish Roman Catholic widow with a daughter, with seal-shooting and a boat and high cliffs right in the young man's way! Lady Scroope could not analyse it, but felt all the danger as though it were by instinct. Partridge and pheasant shooting on a gentleman's own grounds, and an occasional day's hunting with the hounds in his own county, were, in Lady Scroope's estimation, becoming amusements for an English gentleman. They did not interfere with the exercise of his duties. She had by no means brought herself to like the yearly raids into Scotland made latterly by sportsmen. But if Scotch moors and forests were dangerous, what were Irish cliffs! Deer-stalking was bad in her imagination. She was almost sure that when men went up to Scotch forests they did not go to church on Sundays. But the idea of seal-shooting was much more horrible. And then there was that priest who was the only friend of the widow who had the daughter!

On the morning of the day in which Fred was to reach the Manor, Lady Scroope did speak to her husband. "Don't you think, my dear, that something might be done to prevent Fred's returning to that horrid country?"

"What can we do?"

"I suppose he would wish to oblige you. You are being very good to him."

"It is for the old to give, Mary, and for the young to accept. I do all for him because he is all to me; but what am I to him, that he should sacrifice any pleasure for me? He can break my heart. Were I even to quarrel with him, the worst I could do would be to send him to the money-lenders for a year or two."

"But why should he care about his regiment now?"

"Because his regiment means liberty."

"And you won't ask him to give it up?"

"I think not. If I were to ask him I should expect him to yield, and then I should be disappointed were he to refuse. I do not wish him to think me a tyrant." This was the end of the conversation, for Lady Scroope did not as yet dare to speak to the Earl about the widow and her daughter. She must now try her skill and eloquence with the young man himself.

The young man arrived and was received with

kindest greetings. Two horses had preceded him, so that he might find himself mounted as soon as he chose after his arrival, and two others were coming. This was all very well, but his aunt was a little hurt when he declared his purpose of going down to the stables just as she told him that Sophia Mellerby was in the house. He arrived on the 23rd at 4 P.M., and it had been declared that he was to hunt on the morrow. It was already dark, and surely he might have been content on the first evening of his arrival to abstain from the stables! Not a word had been said to Sophie Mellerby of Lady Scroope's future hopes. Lady Scroope and Lady Sophia would each have thought that it was wicked to do so. But the two women had been fussy, and Miss Mellerby must have been less discerning than are young ladies generally, had she not understood what was expected of her. Girls are undoubtedly better prepared to fall in love with men whom they have never seen, than are men with girls. It is a girl's great business in life to love and to be loved. Of some young men it may almost be said that it is their great business to avoid such a catastrophe. Such ought not to have been the case with Fred Neville now; — but in such light he regarded it. He had already said to himself that Sophie Mellerby was to be pitched at his head. He knew no reason, — none as yet, — why he should not like Miss Mellerby well enough. But he was a little on his guard against her, and preferred seeing his horses first. Sophie, when according to custom, and indeed in this instance in accordance with special arrangement, she went into Lady Scroope's sitting-room for tea, was rather disappointed at not finding Mr. Neville there. She knew that he had visited his uncle immediately on his arrival, and having just come in from the park she had gone to her room to make some little preparation for the meeting. If it was written in Fate's book that she was to be the next Lady Scroope, the meeting was important. Perhaps that writing in Fate's book might depend on the very adjustment which she was now making of her hair.

"He has gone to look at his horses," said Lady Scroope, unable not to shew her disappointment by the tone of her voice.

"That is so natural," said Sophie, who was more cunning. "Young men almost idolize their horses. I should like to go and see Dandy whenever he arrives anywhere, only I don't dare!" Dandy was Miss Mellerby's own horse, and was accustomed to make journeys up and down between Mellerby and London.

"I don't think horses and guns and dogs should be too much thought of," said Lady Scroope gravely. "There is a tendency I think at present to give them an undue importance. When our amusements become more serious to us than our business, we must be going astray."

"I suppose we always are going astray," said Miss Mellerby. Lady Scroope sighed and shook her head; but in shaking it she shewed that she completely agreed with the opinion expressed by her guest.

As there were only two horses to be inspected, and as Fred Neville absolutely refused the groom's invitation to look at the old carriage horses belonging to the family, he was back in his aunt's room before Miss Mellerby had gone upstairs to dress for dinner. The introduction was made, and Fred did his best to make himself agreeable. He was such a man that no girl could, at the first sight of him, think herself injured by being asked to love him. She was a good girl, and would have consented to marry no man without feeling sure of his affections; but Fred Neville was bold and frank as well as handsome, and had plenty to say for himself. It might be that he was vicious, or ill-tempered, or selfish, and it would be necessary that she should know much of him before she would give herself into his keeping; but as far as the first sight went, and the first hearing, Sophie Mellerby's impressions were all in Fred's favour. It is no doubt a fact that with the very best of girls a man is placed in a very good light by being heir to a peerage and a large property.

"Do you hunt, Miss Mellerby?" he asked. She shook her head and looked grave, and then laughed. Among her people hunting was not thought to be a desirable accomplishment for young ladies. "Almost all girls do hunt now," said Fred.

"Do you think it is a nice amusement for

young ladies?" asked the aunt in a severe tone.

"I don't see why not; — that is if they know how to ride."

"I know how to ride," said Sophie Mellerby.

"Riding is all very well," said Lady Scroope. "I quite approve of it for girls. When I was young, everybody did not ride as they do now. Nevertheless it is very well, and is thought to be healthy. But as for hunting, Sophie, I'm sure your mamma would be very much distressed if you were to think of such a thing."

"But, dear Lady Scroope, I haven't thought of it, and I am not going to think of it; — and if I thought of it ever so much, I shouldn't do it. Poor mamma would be frightened into fits, — only that nobody at Mellerby could possibly be made to believe it, unless they saw me doing it."

"Then there can be no reason why you shouldn't make the attempt," said Fred. Upon which Lady Scroope pretended to look grave, and told him that he was very wicked. But let an old lady be ever so strict towards her own sex, she likes a little wickedness in a young man, — if only he does not carry it to the extent of marrying the wrong sort of young woman.

Sophia Mellerby was a tall, graceful, well-formed girl, showing her high blood in every line of her face. On her mother's side she had come from the Ancrums, whose family, as everybody knows, is one of the oldest in England; and, as the Earl had said, the Mellerbys had been Mellerbys from the time of King John, and had been living on the same spot for at least four centuries. They were and always had been Mellerbys of Mellerby, — the very name of the parish being the same as that of the family. If Sophia Mellerby did not shew breeding, what girl could shew it? She was fair, with a somewhat thin oval face, with dark eyes, and an almost perfect Grecian nose. Her mouth was small, and her chin delicately formed. And yet it can hardly be said that she was beautiful. Or, if beautiful, she was so in women's eyes rather than in those of men. She lacked colour and perhaps animation in her countenance. She had more character, indeed, than was told by her face, which is generally so true an index of the mind. Her education had been as good as England could afford, and her intellect had been sufficient to enable her to make use of it. But her chief charm in the eyes of many consisted in the fact, doubted by none, that she was every inch a lady. She was an only daughter, too, — with an only brother; and as the Ancrums were all rich, she would have a very pretty fortune of her own. Fred Neville, who had literally been nobody before his cousin had died, might certainly do much worse than marry her.

And after a day or two they did seem to get on very well together. He had reached Scroope on the 21st, and on the 23rd Mrs. Neville arrived with her youngest son Jack Neville. This was rather a trial to the Earl, as he had never yet seen his brother's widow. He had heard when his brother married that she was fast, fond of riding, and loud. She had been the daughter of a Colonel Smith, with whom his brother, at that time a Captain Neville, had formed acquaintance; — and had been a beauty very well known as such at Dublin and other garrison towns. No real harm had ever been known of her, but the old Earl had always felt that his brother had made an unfortunate marriage. As at that time they had not been on speaking terms, it had not signified much; — but there had been a prejudice at Scroope against the Captain's wife, which by no means died out when the late Julia Smith became the Captain's widow with two sons. Old reminiscences remain very firm with old people, — and Lord Scroope was still much afraid of the fast, loud beauty. His principles told him that he should not sever the mother from the son, and that as it suited him to take the son for his own purposes, he should also, to some extent, accept the mother also. But he dreaded the affair. He dreaded Mrs. Neville; and he dreaded Jack, who had been so named after his gallant grandfather, Colonel Smith. When Mrs. Neville arrived, she was found to be so subdued and tame that she could hardly open her mouth before the old Earl. Her loudness, if she ever had been loud, was certainly all gone, — and her fastness, if ever she had been fast, had been worn out of her. She was an old woman, with the relics of great beauty, idolizing her two sons for whom all her life had been a sacrifice, in

45

weak health, and prepared, if necessary, to sit in silent awe at the feet of the Earl who had been so good to her boy.

"I don't know how to thank you for what you have done," she said, in a low voice.

"No thanks are required," said the Earl. "He is the same to us as if he were our own." Then she raised the old man's hand and kissed it, — and the old man owned to himself that he had made a mistake.

As to Jack Neville —. But Jack Neville shall have another chapter opened on his behalf.

Chapter IV.
Jack Neville.

John is a very respectable name; — perhaps there is no name more respectable in the English language. Sir John, as the head of a family, is certainly as respectable as any name can be. For an old family coachman it beats all names. Mr. John Smith would be sure to have a larger balance at his banker's than Charles Smith or Orlando Smith, — or perhaps than any other Smith whatever. The Rev. Frederic Walker might be a wet parson, but the Rev. John Walker would assuredly be a good clergyman at all points, though perhaps a little dull in his sermons. Yet almost all Johns have been Jacks, and Jack, in point of respectability, is the very reverse of John. How it is, or when it is, that the Jacks become re-Johned, and go back to the original and excellent name given to them by their godfathers and godmothers, nobody ever knows. Jack Neville, probably through some foolish fondness on his mother's part, had never been re-Johned, — and consequently the Earl, when he made up his mind to receive his sister-in-law, was at first unwilling to invite his younger nephew. "But he is in the Engineers," said Lady Scroope. The argument had its weight, and Jack Neville was invited. But even that argument failed to obliterate the idea which had taken hold of the Earl's mind. There had never yet been a Jack among the Scroopes.

When Jack came he was found to be very unlike the Nevilles in appearance. In the first place he was dark, and in the next place he was ugly. He was a tall, well-made fellow, taller than his brother, and probably stronger; and he had very different eyes, — very dark brown eyes, deeply set in his head, with large dark eyebrows. He wore his black hair very short, and had no beard whatever. His features were hard, and on one cheek he had a cicatrice, the remains of some misfortune that had happened to him in his boyhood. But in spite of his ugliness, — for he was ugly, there was much about him in his gait and manner that claimed attention. Lord Scroope, the moment that he saw him, felt that he ought not to be called Jack. Indeed the Earl was almost afraid of him, and so after a time was the Countess. "Jack ought to have been the eldest," Fred had said to his aunt.

"Why should he have been the eldest?"

"Because he is so much the cleverest. I could never have got into the Engineers."

"That seems to be a reason why he should be the youngest," said Lady Scroope.

Two or three other people arrived, and the house became much less dull than was its wont.

Jack Neville occasionally rode his brother's horses, and the Earl was forced to acknowledge another mistake. The mother was very silent, but she was a lady. The young Engineer was not only a gentleman, — but for his age a very well educated gentleman, and Lord Scroope was almost proud of his relatives. For the first week the affair between Fred Neville and Miss Mellerby really seemed to make progress. She was not a girl given to flirting, — not prone to outward demonstrations of partiality for a young man; but she never withdrew herself from her intended husband, and Fred seemed quite willing to be attentive. Not a word was said to hurry the young people, and Lady Scroope's hopes were high. Of course no allusion had been made to those horrid Irish people, but it did not seem to Lady Scroope that the heir had left his heart behind him in Co. Clare.

Fred had told his aunt in one of his letters that he would stay three weeks at Scroope, but she had not supposed that he would limit himself exactly to that period. No absolute limit had been fixed for the visit of Mrs. Neville and her younger son, but it was taken for granted that they would not remain should Fred depart. As to Sophie Mellerby, her visit was elastic. She was there for a purpose, and might remain all the winter if the purpose could be so served. For the first fortnight Lady Scroope thought that the affair was progressing well. Fred hunted three days a week, and was occasionally away from home, — going to dine with a regiment at Dorchester, and once making a dash up to London; but his manner to Miss Mellerby was very nice, and there could be no doubt but that Sophie liked him. When, on a sudden, the heir said a word to his aunt which was almost equal to firing a pistol at her head. "I think Master Jack is making it all square with Sophie Mellerby."

If there was anything that Lady Scroope hated almost as much as improper marriages it was slang. She professed that she did not understand it; and in carrying out her profession always stopped the conversation to have any word explained to her which she thought had been used in an improper sense. The idea of a young man making it "all square" with a young woman was repulsive, but the idea of this young man making it "all square" with this young woman was so much more repulsive, and the misery to her was so intensely heightened by the uncon-cern displayed by the heir in so speaking of the girl with whom he ought to have been making it "all square" himself, that she could hardly allow herself to be arrested by that stumbling block. "Impossible!" she exclaimed, — "that is if you mean, — if you mean, — if you mean anything at all."

"I do mean a good deal."

"Then I don't believe a word of it. It's quite out of the question. It's impossible. I'm quite sure your brother understands his position as a gentleman too thoroughly to dream of such a thing."

This was Greek to Fred Neville. Why his brother should not fall in love with a pretty girl, and why a pretty girl should not return the feeling, without any disgrace to his brother, Fred could not understand. His brother was a Neville, and was moreover an uncommonly clever fellow. "Why shouldn't he dream of it?"

"In the first place —. Well! I did think, Fred, that you yourself seemed to be, — seemed to be taken with Miss Mellerby."

"Who? I? Oh, dear no. She's a very nice girl and all that, and I like her amazingly. If she were Jack's wife, I never saw a girl I should so much like for a sister."

"It is quite out of the question. I wonder that you can speak in such a way. What right can your brother have to think of such a girl as Miss Mellerby? He has no position; — no means."

"He is my brother," said Fred, with a little touch of anger, — already discounting his future earldom on his brother's behalf.

"Yes; — he is your brother; but you don't suppose that Mr. Mellerby would give his daughter to an officer in the Engineers who has, as far as I know, no private means whatever."

"He will have, — when my mother dies. Of course I can't speak of doing anything for anybody at present. I may die before my uncle. Nothing is more likely. But then, if I do, Jack would be my uncle's heir."

"I don't believe there's anything in it at all," said Lady Scroope in great dudgeon.

"I dare say not. If there is, they haven't told me. It's not likely they would. But I thought I saw something coming up, and as it seemed to be the most natural thing in the world, I mentioned it. As for me, — Miss Mellerby doesn't care a straw for me. You may be sure of that."

"She would — if you'd ask her."

"But I never shall ask her. What's the use of beating about the bush, aunt? I never shall ask her; and if I did, she wouldn't have me. If you want to make Sophie Mellerby your niece, Jack's your game."

Lady Scroope was ineffably disgusted. To be told that "Jack was her game" was in itself a terrible annoyance to her. But to be so told in reference to such a subject was painful in the extreme. Of course she could not make this young man marry as she wished. She had acknowledged to herself from the first that there could be no cause of anger against him should he not fall into the silken net which was spread for him. Lady Scroope was not an unreasonable woman, and understood well the power which young people have over old people. She knew that she couldn't quarrel with Fred Neville, even if she would. He was the heir, and in a very few years would be the owner of everything. In order to keep him straight, to save him from debts, to protect him from money-lenders, and to secure the family standing and property till he should

52

have made things stable by having a wife and heir of his own, all manner of indulgence must be shown him. She quite understood that such a horse must be ridden with a very light hand. She must put up with slang from him, though she would resent it from any other human being. He must be allowed to smoke in his bedroom, to be late at dinner, to shirk morning prayers, — making her only too happy if he would not shirk Sunday church also. Of course he must choose a bride for himself, — only not a Roman Catholic wild Irish bride of whom nobody knew anything!

As to that other matter concerning Jack and Sophie Mellerby, she could not bring herself to believe it. She had certainly seen that they were good friends, — as would have been quite fit had Fred been engaged to her; but she had not conceived the possibility of any mistake on such a subject. Surely Sophie herself knew better what she was about! How would she, — she, Lady Scroope, — answer it to Lady Sophia, if Sophie should go back to Mellerby from her house, engaged to a younger brother who had nothing but a commission in the Engineers? Sophie had been sent to Scroope on purpose to be fallen in love with by the heir; and how would it be with Lady Scroope if, in lieu of this, she should not only have been fallen in love with by the heir's younger brother, but have responded favourably to so base an affection?

That same afternoon Fred told his uncle that

he was going back to Ireland on the day but one following, thus curtailing his promised three weeks by two days. "I am sorry that you are so much hurried, Fred," said the old man.

"So am I, my lord, — but Johnstone has to go to London on business, and I promised when I got leave that I wouldn't throw him over. You see, — when one has a profession one must attend to it, — more or less."

"But you hardly need the profession."

"Thank you, uncle; — it is very kind of you to say so. And as you wish me to leave it, I will when the year is over. I have told the fellows that I shall stay till next October, and I shouldn't like to change now." The Earl hadn't another word to say.

But on the day before Fred's departure there came a short note from Lady Mary Quin which made poor Lady Scroope more unhappy than ever. Tidings had reached her in a mysterious way that the O'Haras were eagerly expecting the return of Mr. Neville. Lady Mary thought that if Mr. Neville's quarters could be moved from Ennis, it would be very expedient for many reasons. She knew that enquiries had been made for him and that he was engaged to dine on a certain day with Father Marty the priest. Father Marty would no doubt go any lengths to serve his friends the O'Haras. Then Lady Mary was very anxious that not a word should be said to Mr. Neville which might lead him to suppose that reports respecting him were being sent from

Quin Castle to Scroope.

The Countess in her agony thought it best to tell the whole story to the Earl. "But what can I do?" said the old man. "Young men will form these acquaintances." His fears were evidently as yet less dark than those of his wife.

"It would be very bad if we were to hear that he was married to a girl of whom we only know that she is a Roman Catholic and friendless."

The Earl's brow became very black. "I don't think that he would treat me in that way."

"Not meaning it, perhaps; — but if he should become entangled and make a promise!"

Then the Earl did speak to his nephew. "Fred," he said, "I have been thinking a great deal about you. I have little else to think of now. I should take it as a mark of affection from you if you would give up the army — at once."

"And not join my regiment again at all?"

"It is absurd that you should do so in your present position. You should be here, and learn the circumstances of the property before it becomes your own. There can hardly be more than a year or two left for the lesson."

The Earl's manner was very impressive. He looked into his nephew's face as he spoke, and stood with his hand upon the young man's shoulder. But Fred Neville was a Neville all over, — and the Nevilles had always chosen to have their own way. He had not the power of intellect nor the finished manliness which his brother possessed; but he could be as obstinate as any

Neville, — as obstinate as his father had been, or his uncle. And in this matter he had arguments which his uncle could hardly answer on the spur of the moment. No doubt he could sell out in proper course, but at the present moment he was as much bound by military law to return as would be any common soldier at the expiration of his furlough. He must go back. That at any rate was certain. And if his uncle did not much mind it, he would prefer to remain with his regiment till October.

Lord Scroope could not condescend to repeat his request, or even again to allude to it. His whole manner altered as he took his hand away from his nephew's shoulder. But still he was determined that there should be no quarrel. As yet there was no ground for quarrelling, — and by any quarrel the injury to him would be much greater than any that could befall the heir. He stood for a moment and then he spoke again in a tone very different from that he had used before. "I hope," he said, — and then he paused again; "I hope you know how very much depends on your marrying in a manner suitable to your position."

"Quite so; — I think."

"It is the one hope left to me to see you properly settled in life."

"Marriage is a very serious thing, uncle. Suppose I were not to marry at all! Sometimes I think my brother is much more like marrying than I am."

"You are bound to marry," said the Earl solemnly. "And you are specially bound by every duty to God and man to make no marriage that will be disgraceful to the position which you are called upon to fill."

"At any rate I will not do that," said Fred Neville proudly. From this the Earl took some comfort, and then the interview was over.

On the day appointed by himself Fred left the Manor, and his mother and brother went on the following day. But after he was gone, on that same afternoon, Jack Neville asked Sophie Mellerby to be his wife. She refused him, — with all the courtesy she knew how to use, but also with all the certainty. And as soon as he had left the house she told Lady Scroope what had happened.

CHAPTER V.
ARDKILL COTTAGE.

The cliffs of Moher in Co. Clare, on the western coast of Ireland, are not as well known to tourists as they should be. It may be doubted whether Lady Mary Quin was right when she called them the highest cliffs in the world, but they are undoubtedly very respectable cliffs, and run up some six hundred feet from the sea as nearly perpendicular as cliffs should be. They are beautifully coloured, streaked with yellow veins, and with great masses of dark red rock; and beneath them lies the broad and blue Atlantic. Lady Mary's exaggeration as to the comparative height is here acknowledged, but had she said that below them rolls the brightest bluest clearest water in the world she would not have been far wrong. To the south of these cliffs there runs inland a broad bay, — Liscannor bay, on the sides of which are two little villages, Liscannor and Lahinch. At the latter, Fred Neville, since he had been quartered at Ennis, had kept a boat for the sake of shooting seals and exploring the coast, — and generally carrying out his spirit of adventure. Not far from Liscannor was

Castle Quin, the seat of the Earl of Kilfenora; and some way up from Liscannor towards the cliffs, about two miles from the village, there is a cottage called Ardkill. Here lived Mrs. and Miss O'Hara.

It was the nearest house to the rocks, from which it was distant less than half a mile. The cottage, so called, was a low rambling long house, but one storey high, — very unlike an English cottage. It stood in two narrow lengths, the one running at right angles to the other; and contained a large kitchen, two sitting rooms, — of which one was never used, — and four or five bed-rooms of which only three were furnished. The servant girl occupied one, and the two ladies the others. It was a blank place enough, — and most unlike that sort of cottage which English ladies are supposed to inhabit, when they take to cottage life. There was no garden to it, beyond a small patch in which a few potatoes were planted. It was so near to the ocean, so exposed to winds from the Atlantic, that no shrubs would live there. Everything round it, even the herbage, was impregnated with salt, and told tales of the neighbouring waves. When the wind was from the west the air would be so laden with spray that one could not walk there without being wet. And yet the place was very healthy, and noted for the fineness of its air. Rising from the cottage, which itself stood high, was a steep hill running up to the top of the cliff, covered with that peculiar moss which the salt spray of the ocean produces. On this side the land was altogether open, but a few sheep were always grazing there when the wind was not so high as to drive them to some shelter. Behind the cottage there was an enclosed paddock which belonged to it, and in which Mrs. O'Hara kept her cow. Roaming free around the house, and sometimes in it, were a dozen hens and a noisy old cock which, with the cow, made up the total of the widow's live stock. About a half a mile from the cottage on the way to Liscannor there were half a dozen mud cabins which contained Mrs. O'Hara's nearest neighbours, — and an old burying ground. Half a mile further on again was the priest's house, and then on to Liscannor there were a few other straggling cabins here and there along the road.

Up to the cottage indeed there could hardly be said to be more than a track, and beyond the cottage no more than a sheep path. The road coming out from Liscannor was a real road as far as the burying ground, but from thence onward it had degenerated. A car, or carriage if needed, might be brought up to the cottage door, for the ground was hard and the way was open. But no wheels ever travelled there now. The priest, when he would come, came on horseback, and there was a shed in which he could tie up his nag. He himself from time to time would send up a truss of hay for his nag's use, and would think himself cruelly used because the cow would find her way in and eat it. No other horse ever called at the widow's door. What slender stores were needed for her use, were all brought on the girls' backs from Liscannor. To the north of the cottage, along the cliff, there was no road for miles, nor was there house or habitation. Castle Quin, in which the noble but somewhat impoverished Quin family lived nearly throughout the year, was distant, inland, about three miles from the cottage. Lady Mary had said in her letter to her friend that Mrs. O'Hara was a lady; — and as Mrs. O'Hara had no other neighbour, ranking with herself in that respect, so near her, and none other but the Protestant clergyman's wife within six miles of her, charity, one would have thought, might have induced some of the Quin family to notice her. But the Quins were Protestant, and Mrs. O'Hara was not only a Roman Catholic, but a Roman Catholic who had been brought into the parish by the priest. No evil certainly was known of her, but then nothing was known of her; and the Quins were a very cautious people where religion was called in question. In the days of the famine Father Marty and the Earl and the Protestant vicar had worked together in the good cause; — but those days were now gone by, and the strange intimacy had soon died away. The Earl when he met the priest would bow to him, and the two clergymen would bow to each other; — but beyond such dumb salutation there was no intercourse between them. It had been held therefore to be impossible to take any notice of

61

the priest's friends.

And what notice could have been taken of two ladies who came from nobody knew where, to live in that wild out-of-the-way place, nobody knew why? They called themselves mother and daughter, and they called themselves O'Haras; — but there was no evidence of the truth even of these assertions. They were left therefore in their solitude, and never saw the face of a friend across their door step except that of Father Marty.

In truth Mrs. O'Hara's life had been of a nature almost to necessitate such solitude. With her story we have nothing to do here. For our purpose there is no need that her tale should be told. Suffice it to say that she had been deserted by her husband, and did not now know whether she was or was not a widow. This was in truth the only mystery attached to her. She herself was an Englishwoman, though a Catholic; but she had been left early an orphan, and had been brought up in a provincial town of France by her grandmother. There she had married a certain Captain O'Hara, she having some small means of her own sufficient to make her valuable in the eyes of an adventurer. At that time she was no more than eighteen, and had given her hand to the Captain in opposition to the wishes of her only guardian. What had been her life from that time to the period at which, under Father Marty's auspices, she became the inhabitant of Ardkill Cottage, no one knew but herself.

She was then utterly dissevered from all friends and relatives, and appeared on the western coast of County Clare with her daughter, a perfect stranger to every one. Father Marty was an old man, now nearly seventy, and had been educated in France. There he had known Mrs. O'Hara's grandmother, and hence had arisen the friendship which had induced him to bring the lady into his parish. She came there with a daughter, then hardly more than a child. Between two and three years had passed since her coming, and the child was now a grown-up girl, nearly nineteen years old. Of her means little or nothing was known accurately, even to the priest. She had told him that she had saved enough out of the wreck on which to live with her girl after some very humble fashion, and she paid her way. There must have come some sudden crash, or she would hardly have taken her child from an expensive Parisian school to vegetate in such solitude as that she had chosen. And it was a solitude from which there seemed to be no chance of future escape. They had brought with them a piano and a few books, mostly French; — and with these it seemed to have been intended that the two ladies should make their future lives endurable. Other resources except such as the scenery of the cliffs afforded them, they had none.

The author would wish to impress upon his readers, if it may be possible, some idea of the outward appearance and personal character of each of these two ladies, as his story can hardly be told successfully unless he do so. The elder, who was at this time still under forty years of age, would have been a very handsome woman had not troubles, suffering, and the contests of a rugged life, in which she had both endured and dared much, given to her face a look of hard combative resolution which was not feminine. She was rather below than above the average height, — or at any rate looked to be so, as she was strongly made, with broad shoulders, and a waist that was perhaps not now as slender as when she first met Captain O'Hara. But her hair was still black, — as dark at least as hair can be which is not in truth black at all but only darkly brown. Whatever might be its colour there was no tinge of grey upon it. It was glossy, silken, and long as when she was a girl. I do not think that she took pride in it. How could she take pride in personal beauty, when she was never seen by any man younger than Father Marty or the old peasant who brought turf to her door in creels on a donkey's back? But she wore it always without any cap, tied in a simple knot behind her head. Whether chignons had been invented then the author does not remember, — but they certainly had not become common on the coast of County Clare, and the peasants about Liscannor thought Mrs. O'Hara's head of hair the finest they had ever seen. Had the ladies Quin of the Castle possessed such hair as that, they would not have been the ladies Quin to this day.

Her eyes were lustrous, dark, and very large, — beautiful eyes certainly; but they were eyes that you might fear. They had been softer perhaps in youth, before the spirit of the tiger had been roused in the woman's bosom by neglect and ill-usage. Her face was now bronzed by years and weather. Of her complexion she took no more care than did the neighbouring fishermen of theirs, and the winds and the salt water, and perhaps the working of her own mind, had told upon it, to make it rough and dark. But yet there was a colour in her cheeks, as we often see in those of wandering gipsies, which would make a man stop to regard her who had eyes appreciative of beauty. Her nose was well formed, — a heaven-made nose, and not a lump of flesh stuck on to the middle of her face as women's noses sometimes are; — but it was somewhat short and broad at the nostrils, a nose that could imply much anger, and perhaps tenderness also. Her face below her nose was very short. Her mouth was large, but laden with expression. Her lips were full and her teeth perfect as pearls. Her chin was short and perhaps now verging to that size which we call a double chin, and marked by as broad a dimple as ever Venus made with her finger on the face of a woman.

She had ever been strong and active, and years in that retreat had told upon her not at all. She would still walk to Liscannor, and thence round, when the tide was low, beneath the cliffs, and up by a path which the boys had made from the foot through the rocks to the summit, though the distance was over ten miles, and the ascent was very steep. She would remain for hours on the rocks, looking down upon the sea, when the weather was almost at its roughest. When the winds were still, and the sun was setting across the ocean, and the tame waves were only just audible as they rippled on the stones below, she would sit there with her child, holding the girl's hand or just touching her arm, and would be content so to stay almost without a word; but when the winds blew, and the heavy spray came up in blinding volumes, and the white-headed sea-monsters were roaring in their fury against the rocks, she would be there alone with her hat in her hand, and her hair drenched. She would watch the gulls wheeling and floating beneath her, and would listen to their screams and try to read their voices. She would envy the birds as they seemed to be worked into madness by the winds which still were not strong enough to drive them from their purposes. To linger there among the rocks seemed to be the only delight left to her in life, — except that intense delight which a mother has in loving her child. She herself read but little, and never put a hand upon the piano. But she had a faculty of sitting and thinking, of brooding over her own past years and dreaming of her daughter's future life, which never deserted her. With her the days were doubtless very sad, but it cannot truly be said that they were dull or tedious.

And there was a sparkle of humour about her too, which would sometimes shine the brightest when there was no one by her to appreciate it. Her daughter would smile at her mother's sallies, — but she did so simply in kindness. Kate did not share her mother's sense of humour, — did not share it as yet. With the young the love of fun is gratified generally by grotesque movement. It is not till years are running on that the grotesqueness of words and ideas is appreciated. But Mrs. O'Hara would expend her art on the household drudge, or on old Barney Corcoran who came with the turf, — though by neither of them was she very clearly understood. Now and again she would have a war of words with the priest, and that, I think, she liked. She was intensely combative, if ground for a combat arose; and would fight on any subject with any human being — except her daughter. And yet with the priest she never quarrelled; and though she was rarely beaten in her contests with him, she submitted to him in much. In matters touching her religion she submitted to him altogether.

Kate O'Hara was in face very like her mother; — strangely like, for in much she was very different. But she had her mother's eyes, — though hers were much softer in their lustre, as became her youth, — and she had her mother's nose, but without that look of scorn which would come upon her mother's face when the nostrils were inflated. And in that peculiar shortness of the lower face she was the very echo of her mother. But the mouth was smaller, the lips less full, and the dimple less exaggerated. It was a fairer face to look upon, — fairer, perhaps, than her mother's had ever been; but it was less expressive, and in it there was infinitely less capability for anger, and perhaps less capability for the agonising extremes of tenderness. But Kate was taller than her mother, and seemed by her mother's side to be slender. Nevertheless she was strong and healthy; and though she did not willingly join in those longer walks, or expose herself to the weather as did her mother, there was nothing feeble about her, nor was she averse to action. Life at Ardkill Cottage was dull, and therefore she also was dull. Had she been surrounded by friends, such as she had known in her halcyon school days at Paris, she would have been the gayest of the gay.

Her hair was dark as her mother's, — even darker. Seen by the side of Miss O'Hara's, the mother's hair was certainly not black, but one could hardly think that hair could be blacker than the daughter's. But hers fell in curling clusters round her neck, — such clusters as now one never sees. She would shake them in sport, and the room would seem to be full of her locks. But she used to say herself to her mother that there was already to be found a grey hair among them now and again, and she would at times shew one, declaring that she would be an old woman before her mother was middle-aged.

Her life at Ardkill Cottage was certainly very

dull. Memory did but little for her, and she hardly knew how to hope. She would read, till she had nearly learned all their books by heart, and would play such tunes as she knew by the hour together, till the poor instrument, subject to the sea air and away from any tuner's skill, was discordant with its limp strings. But still, with all this, her mind would become vacant and weary. "Mother," she would say, "is it always to be like this?"

"Not always, Kate," the mother once answered.

"And when will it be changed?"

"In a few days, — in a few hours, Kate."

"What do you mean, mother?"

"That eternity is coming, with all its glory and happiness. If it were not so, it would, indeed, be very bad."

It may be doubted whether any human mind has been able to content itself with hopes of eternity, till distress in some shape has embittered life. The preachers preach very well, — well enough to leave many convictions on the minds of men; but not well enough to leave that conviction. And godly men live well, — but we never see them living as though such were their conviction. And were it so, who would strive and moil in this world? When the heart has been broken, and the spirit ground to the dust by misery, then, — such is God's mercy — eternity suffices to make life bearable. When Mrs. O'Hara spoke to her daughter of eternity, there was but cold comfort in the word. The girl wanted something here, — pleasures, companions, work, perhaps a lover. This had happened before Lieutenant Neville of the 20th Hussars had been seen in those parts.

And the mother herself, in speaking as she had spoken, had, perhaps unintentionally, indulged in a sarcasm on life which the daughter certainly had not been intended to understand. "Yes; — it will always be like this for you, for you, unfortunate one that you are. There is no other further look-out in this life. You are one of the wretched to whom the world offers nothing; and therefore, — as, being human, you must hope, — build your hopes on eternity." Had the words been read clearly, that would have been their true meaning. What could she do for her child? Bread and meat, with a roof over her head, and raiment which sufficed for life such as theirs, she could supply. The life would have been well enough had it been their fate, and within their power, to earn the bread and meat, the shelter and the raiment. But to have it, and without work, — to have that, and nothing more, in absolute idleness, was such misery that there was no resource left but eternity!

And yet the mother when she looked at her daughter almost persuaded herself that it need not be so. The girl was very lovely, — so lovely that, were she but seen, men would quarrel for her as to who should have her in his keeping. Such beauty, such life, such capability for giving and receiving enjoyment could not have been intended to wither on a lone cliff over the Atlantic! There must be fault somewhere. But yet to live had been the first necessity; and life in cities, among the haunts of men, had been impossible with such means as this woman possessed. When she had called her daughter to her, and had sought peace under the roof which her friend the priest had found for her, peace and a roof to shelter her had been the extent of her desires. To be at rest, and independent, with her child within her arms, had been all that the woman asked of the gods. For herself it sufficed. For herself she was able to acknowledge that the rest which she had at least obtained was infinitely preferable to the unrest of her past life. But she soon learned, — as she had not expected to learn before she made the experiment, — that that which was to her peace, was to her daughter life within a tomb. "Mother, is it always to be like this?"

Had her child not carried the weight of good blood, had some small grocer or country farmer been her father, she might have come down to the neighbouring town of Ennistimon, and found a fitting mate there. Would it not have been better so? From that weight of good blood, — or gift, if it please us to call it, — what advantage would ever come to her girl? It can not really be that all those who swarm in the world below the bar of gentlehood are less blessed, or intended to be less blessed, than the few who float in the higher air. As to real blessedness, does it not come from fitness to the outer life and a sense of duty that shall produce such fitness? Does any one believe that the Countess has a greater share of happiness than the grocer's wife, or is less subject to the miseries which flesh inherits? But such matters cannot be changed by the will. This woman could not bid her daughter go and meet the butcher's son on equal terms, or seek her friends among the milliners of the neighbouring town. The burden had been imposed and must be borne, even though it isolated them from all the world.

"Mother, is it always to be like this?" Of course the mother knew what was needed. It was needed that the girl should go out into the world and pair, that she should find some shoulder on which she might lean, some arm that would be strong to surround her, the heart of some man and the work of some man to which she might devote herself. The girl, when she asked her question, did not know this, — but the mother knew it. The mother looked at her child and said that of all living creatures her child was surely the loveliest. Was it not fit that she should go forth and be loved; — that she should at any rate go forth and take her chance with others? But how should such going forth be managed? And then, — were there not dangers, terrible dangers, — dangers specially terrible to one so friendless as her child? Had not she herself been wrecked among the rocks, trusting herself to one who had been utterly unworthy, — loving one who had been utterly unlovely? Men so often are as ravenous wolves, merciless, rapacious, without hearts, full of greed, full of lust, looking on female beauty as prey, regarding the love of woman and her very life as a toy! Were she higher in the world there might be safety. Were she lower there might be safety. But how could she send her girl forth into the world without sending her certainly among the wolves? And yet that piteous question was always sounding in her ears. "Mother, is it always to be like this?"

Then Lieutenant Neville had appeared upon the scene, dressed in a sailor's jacket and trowsers, with a sailor's cap upon his head, with a loose handkerchief round his neck and his hair blowing to the wind. In the eyes of Kate O'Hara he was an Apollo. In the eyes of any girl he must have seemed to be as good-looking a fellow as ever tied a sailor's knot. He had made acquaintance with Father Marty at Liscannor, and the priest had dined with him at Ennis. There had been a return visit, and the priest, perhaps innocently, had taken him up on the cliffs. There he had met the two ladies, and our hero had been introduced to Kate O'Hara.

Chapter VI.
I'll Go Bail She Likes It.

It might be that the young man was a ravenous wolf, but his manners were not wolfish. Had Mrs. O'Hara been a princess, supreme in her own rights, young Neville could not have treated her or her daughter with more respect. At first Kate had wondered at him, but had said but little. She had listened to him, as he talked to her mother and the priest about the cliffs and the birds and the seals he had shot, and she had felt that it was this, something like this, that was needed to make life so sweet that as yet there need be no longing, no thought, for eternity. It was not that all at once she loved him, but she felt that he was a thing to love. His very appearance on the cliff, and the power of thinking of him when he was gone, for a while banished all tedium from her life. "Why should you shoot the poor gulls?" That was the first question she asked him; and she asked it hardly in tenderness to the birds, but because with the unconscious cunning of her sex she understood that tenderness in a woman is a charm in the eyes of a man.

"Only because it is so difficult to get at them,"

said Fred. "I believe there is no other reason, — except that one must shoot something."

"But why must you?" asked Mrs. O'Hara.

"To justify one's guns. A man takes to shooting as a matter of course. It's a kind of institution. There ain't any tigers, and so we shoot birds. And in this part of the world there ain't any pheasants, and so we shoot sea-gulls."

"Excellently argued," said the priest.

"Or rather one don't, for it's impossible to get at them. But I'll tell you what, Father Marty," — Neville had already assumed the fashion of calling the priest by his familiar priestly name, as strangers do much more readily than they who belong to the country, — "I'll tell you what, Father Marty, — I've shot one of the finest seals I ever saw, and if Morony can get him at low water, I'll send the skin up to Mrs. O'Hara."

"And send the oil to me," said the priest. "There's some use in shooting a seal. But you can do nothing with those birds, — unless you get enough of their feathers to make a bed."

This was in October, and before the end of November Fred Neville was, after a fashion, intimate at the cottage. He had never broken bread at Mrs. O'Hara's table; nor, to tell the truth, had any outspoken, clearly intelligible word of love been uttered by him to the girl. But he had been seen with them often enough, and the story had become sufficiently current at Liscannor to make Lady Mary Quin think that she was justified in sending her bad news to her

75

friend Lady Scroope. This she did not do till Fred had been induced, with some difficulty, to pass a night at Castle Quin. Lady Mary had not scrupled to ask a question about Miss O'Hara, and had thought the answer very unsatisfactory. "I don't know what makes them live there, I'm sure. I should have thought you would have known that," replied Neville, in answer to her question.

"They are perfect mysteries to us," said Lady Mary.

"I think that Miss O'Hara is the prettiest girl I ever saw in my life," said Fred boldly, "and I should say the handsomest woman, if it were not that there may be a question between her and her mother."

"You are enthusiastic," said Lady Mary Quin, and after that the letter to Scroope was written.

In the meantime the seal-skin was cured, — not perhaps in the very best fashion, and was sent up to Miss O'Hara, with Mr. Neville's compliments. The skin of a seal that has been shot by the man and not purchased is a present that any lady may receive from any gentleman. The most prudent mamma that ever watched over her dovecote with Argus eyes, permitting no touch of gallantry to come near it, could hardly insist that a seal-skin in the rough should be sent back to the donor. Mrs. O'Hara was by no means that most prudent mamma, and made, not only the seal-skin, but the donor also welcome. Must it not be that by some chance advent such as this that the change must be effected in her girl's life, should any change ever be made? And her girl was good. Why should she fear for her? The man had been brought there by her only friend, the priest, and why should she fear him? And yet she did fear; and though her face was never clouded when her girl spoke of the new comer, though she always mentioned Captain Neville's name as though she herself liked the man, though she even was gracious to him when he shewed himself near the cottage, — still there was a deep dread upon her when her eyes rested upon him, when her thoughts flew to him. Men are wolves to women, and utterly merciless when feeding high their lust. 'Twas thus her own thoughts shaped themselves, though she never uttered a syllable to her daughter in disparagement of the man. This was the girl's chance. Was she to rob her of it? And yet, of all her duties, was not the duty of protecting her girl the highest and the dearest that she owned? If the man meant well by her girl, she would wash his feet with her hair, kiss the hem of his garments, and love the spot on which she had first seen him stand like a young sea-god. But if evil, — if he meant evil to her girl, if he should do evil to her Kate, — then she knew that there was so much of the tiger within her bosom as would serve to rend him limb from limb. With such thoughts as these she had hardly ever left them together. Nor had such leaving together seemed to be desired by them. As for

Kate she certainly would have shunned it. She thought of Fred Neville during all her waking moments, and dreamed of him at night. His coming had certainly been to her as the coming of a god. Though he did not appear on the cliffs above once or twice a week, and had done so but for a few weeks, his presence had altered the whole tenour of her life. She never asked her mother now whether it was to be always like this. There was a freshness about her life which her mother understood at once. She was full of play, reading less than was her wont, but still with no sense of tedium. Of the man in his absence she spoke but seldom, and when his name was on her lips she would jest with it, — as though the coming of a young embryo lord to shoot gulls on their coast was quite a joke. The seal-skin which he had given her was very dear to her, and she was at no pains to hide her liking; but of the man as a lover she had never seemed to think.

Nor did she think of him as a lover. It is not by such thinking that love grows. Nor did she ever tell herself that while he was there, coming on one day and telling them that his boat would be again there on another, life was blessed to her, and that, therefore, when he should have left them, her life would be accursed to her. She knew nothing of all this. But yet she thought of him, and dreamed of him, and her young head was full of little plans with every one of which he was connected.

And it may almost be said that Fred Neville was as innocent in the matter as was the girl. It is true, indeed, that men are merciless as wolves to women, — that they become so, taught by circumstances and trained by years; but the young man who begins by meaning to be a wolf must be bad indeed. Fred Neville had no such meaning. On his behalf it must be acknowledged that he had no meaning whatever when he came again and again to Ardkill. Had he examined himself in the matter he would have declared that he liked the mother quite as well as the daughter. When Lady Mary Quin had thrown at him her very blunt arrow he had defended himself on that plea. Accident, and the spirit of adventure, had thrust these ladies in his path, and no doubt he liked them the better because they did not live as other people lived. Their solitude, the close vicinity of the ocean, the feeling that in meeting them none of the ordinary conventional usages of society were needed, the wildness and the strangeness of the scene, all had charms which he admitted to himself. And he knew that the girl was very lovely. Of course he said so to himself and to others. To take delight in beauty is assumed to be the nature of a young man, and this young man was not one to wish to differ from others in that respect. But when he went back to spend his Christmas at Scroope, he had never told even himself that he intended to be her lover.

"Good-bye, Mrs. O'Hara," he said, a day or

two before he left Ennis.

"So you're going?"

"Oh yes, I'm off. The orders from home are imperative. One has to cut one's lump of Christmas beef and also one's lump of Christmas pudding. It is our family religion, you know."

"What a happiness to have a family to visit!"

"It's all very well, I suppose. I don't grumble. Only it's a bore going away, somehow."

"You are coming back to Ennis?" asked Kate.

"Coming back; — I should think so. Barney Morony wouldn't be quite so quiet if I was not coming back. I'm to dine with Father Marty at Liscannor on the 15th of January, to meet another priest from Milltown Malbay, — the best fellow in the world he says."

"That's Father Creech; — not half such a good fellow, Mr. Neville, as Father Marty himself."

"He couldn't be better. However, I shall be here then, and if I have any luck you shall have another skin of the same size by that time." Then he shook hands with them both, and there was a feeling that the time would be blank till he should be again there in his sailor's jacket.

When the second week in January had come Mrs. O'Hara heard that the gallant young officer of the 20th was back in Ennis, and she well remembered that he had told her of his intention to dine with the priest. On the Sunday she saw Mr. Marty after mass, and managed to have a few words with him on the road while Kate returned to the cottage alone. "So your friend

Mr. Neville has come back to Ennis," she said.

"I didn't know that he had come. He promised to dine with me on Thursday, — only I think nothing of promises from these young fellows."

"He told me he was to be with you."

"More power to him. He'll be welcome. I'm getting to be a very ould man, Misthress O'Hara; but I'm not so ould but I like to have the young ones near me."

"It is pleasant to see a bright face like his."

"That's thrue for you, Misthress O'Hara. I like to see 'em bright and ganial. I don't know that I ever shot so much as a sparrow, meself, but I love to hear them talk of their shootings, and huntings, and the like of that. I've taken a fancy to that boy, and he might do pretty much as he plazes wid me."

"And I too have taken a fancy to him, Father Marty."

"Shure and how could you help it?"

"But he mustn't do as he pleases with me." Father Marty looked up into her face as though he did not understand her. "If I were alone, as you are, I could afford, like you, to indulge in the pleasure of a bright face. Only in that case he would not care to let me see it."

"Bedad thin, Misthress O'Hara, I don't know a fairer face to look on in all Corcomroe than your own, — that is when you're not in your tantrums, Misthress O'Hara." The priest was a privileged person, and could say what he liked to his friend; and she understood that a priest

81

might say without fault what would be very faulty if it came from any one else.

"I'm in earnest now, Father Marty. What shall we do if our darling Kate thinks of this young man more than is good for her?" Father Marty raised his hat and began to scratch his head. "If you like to look at the fair face of a handsome lad —"

"I do thin, Misthress O'Hara."

"Must not she like it also?"

"I'll go bail she likes it," said the priest.

"And what will come next?"

"I'll tell you what it is, Misthress O'Hara. Would you want to keep her from even seeing a man at all?"

"God forbid."

"It's not the way to make them happy, nor yet safe. If it's to be that way wid her, she'd better be a nun all out; and I'd be far from proposing that to your Kate."

"She is hardly fit for so holy a life."

"And why should she? I niver like seeing too many of 'em going that way, and them that are prittiest are the last I'd send there. But if not a nun, it stands to reason she must take chance with the rest of 'em. She's been too much shut up already. Let her keep her heart till he asks her for it; but if he does ask her, why shouldn't she be his wife? How many of them young officers take Irish wives home with 'em every year. Only for them, our beauties wouldn't have a chance."

CHAPTER VII.
FATHER MARTY'S HOSPITALITY.

Such was the philosophy, or, perhaps, it may be better said such was the humanity of Father Marty! But in encouraging Mrs. O'Hara to receive this dangerous visitor he had by no means spoken without consideration. In one respect we must abandon Father Marty to the judgment and censure of fathers and mothers. The whole matter looked at from Lady Scroope's point of view was no doubt very injurious to the priest's character. He regarded a stranger among them, such as was Fred Neville, as fair spoil, as a Philistine to seize whom and capture him for life on behalf of any Irish girl would be a great triumph; — a spoiling of the Egyptian to the accomplishment of which he would not hesitate to lend his priestly assistance, the end to be accomplished, of course, being marriage. For Lord Scroope and his family and his blood and his religious fanaticism he could entertain no compassion whatever. Father Marty was no great politician, and desired no rebellion against England. Even in the days of O'Connell and repeal he had been but luke-warm. But justice for Ireland in the guise of wealthy English husbands for pretty Irish girls he desired with all his heart. He was true to his own faith, to the backbone, but he entertained no prejudice against a good looking Protestant youth when a fortunate marriage was in question. So little had been given to the Irish in these days, that they were bound to take what they could get. Lord Scroope and the Countess, had they known the priest's views on this matter, would have regarded him as an unscrupulous intriguing ruffian, prepared to destroy the happiness of a noble family by a wicked scheme. But his views of life, as judged from the other side, admitted of some excuse. As for a girl breaking her heart, he did not, perhaps, much believe in such a catastrophe. Of a sore heart a girl must run the chance, — as also must a man. That young men do go about promising marriage and not keeping their promise, he knew well. None could know that better than he did, for he was the repository of half the love secrets in his parish. But all that was part of the evil coming from the fall of Adam, and must be endured till, — till the Pope should have his own again, and be able to set all things right. In the meantime young women must do the best they could to keep their lovers; — and should one lover break away, then must the deserted one use her experience towards getting a second. But how was a girl to have a lover at all, if she were never allowed to see a man? He had been bred a priest from his youth upwards, and knew nothing of love; but nevertheless it was a pain to him to see a young girl, good-looking, healthy, fit to be the mother of children, pine away, unsought for, uncoupled, — as it would be a pain to see a fruit grow ripe upon the tree, and then fall and perish for the want of plucking. His philosophy was perhaps at fault, and it may be that his humanity was unrefined. But he was human to the core, — and, at any rate, unselfish. That there might be another danger was a fact that he looked full in the face. But what victory can be won without danger? And he thought that he knew this girl, who three times a year would open her whole heart to him in confession. He was sure that she was not only innocent, but good. And of the man, too, he was prone to believe good; — though who on such a question ever trusts a man's goodness? There might be danger and there must be discretion; but surely it would not be wise, because evil was possible, that such a one as Kate O'Hara should be kept from all that intercourse without which a woman is only half a woman! He had considered it all, though the reader may perhaps think that as a minister of the gospel he had come to a strange conclusion. He himself, in his own defence, would have said that having served many years in the ministry he had learned to know the nature of men and women.

Mrs. O'Hara said not a word to Kate of the doctrines which the priest had preached, but she found herself encouraged to mention their new friend's name to the girl. During Fred's absence hardly a word had been spoken concerning him in the cottage. Mrs. O'Hara had feared the subject, and Kate had thought of him much too often to allow his name to be on her tongue. But now as they sat after dinner over their peat fire the mother began the subject. "Mr. Neville is to dine with Father Marty on Thursday."

"Is he, mother?"

"Barney Morony was telling me that he was back at Ennis. Barney had to go in and see him about the boat."

"He won't go boating such weather as this, mother?"

"It seems that he means it. The winds are not so high now as they were in October, and the men understand well when the sea will be high."

"It is frightful to think of anybody being in one of those little boats now." Kate ever since she had lived in these parts had seen the canoes from Liscannor and Lahinch about in the bay, summer and winter, and had never found anything dreadful in it before.

"I suppose he'll come up here again," said the mother; but to this Kate made no answer. "He is to sleep at Father Marty's I fancy, and he can hardly do that without paying us a visit."

"The days are short and he'll want all his time for the boating," said Kate with a little pout.

"He'll find half-an-hour, I don't doubt. Shall you be glad to see him, Kate?"

86

"I don't know, mother. One is glad almost to see any one up here. It's as good as a treat when old Corcoran comes up with the turf."

"But Mr. Neville is not like old Corcoran, Kate."

"Not in the least, mother. I do like Mr. Neville better than Corcoran, because you see with Corcoran the excitement is very soon over. And Corcoran hasn't very much to say for himself."

"And Mr. Neville has?"

"He says a great deal more to you than he does to me, mother."

"I like him very much. I should like him very much indeed if there were no danger in his coming."

"What danger?"

"That he should steal your heart away, my own, my darling, my child." Then Kate, instead of answering, got up and threw herself at her mother's knees, and buried her face in her mother's lap, and Mrs. O'Hara knew that that act of larceny had already been perpetrated.

And how should it have been otherwise? But of such stealing it is always better that no mention should be made till the theft has been sanctified by free gift. Till the loss has been spoken of and acknowledged, it may in most cases be recovered. Had Neville never returned from Scroope, and his name never been mentioned by the mother to her daughter, it may be that Kate O'Hara would not have known that she had loved him. For a while she would have been sad. For a month or two, as she lay wakeful in her bed she would have thought of her dreams. But she would have thought of them as only dreams. She would have been sure that she could have loved him had any fair ending been possible for such love; but she would have assured herself that she had been on her guard, and that she was safe in spite of her dreams. But now the flame in her heart had been confessed and in some degree sanctioned, and she would foster it rather than quench it. Even should such a love be capable of no good fortune, would it not be better to have a few weeks of happy dreaming than a whole life that should be passionless? What could she do with her own heart there, living in solitude, with none but the sea gulls to look at her? Was it not infinitely better that she should give it away to such a young god as this than let it feed upon itself miserably? Yes, she would give it away; — but might it not be that the young god would not take the gift?

On the third day after his arrival at Ennis, Neville was at Liscannor with the priest. He little dreamed that the fact of his dining and sleeping at Father Marty's house would be known to the ladies at Castle Quin, and communicated from them to his aunt at Scroope Manor. Not that he would have been deterred from accepting the priest's hospitality or frightened into accepting that of the noble owner of the castle, had he known precisely all that would be written about it. He would not have altered his conduct in a

88

matter in which he considered himself entitled to regulate it, in obedience to any remonstrances from Scroope Manor. Objections to the society of a Roman Catholic priest because of his religion he would have regarded as old-fashioned fanaticism. As for Earls and their daughters he would no doubt have enough of them in his future life, and this special Earl and his daughters had not fascinated him. He had chosen to come to Ireland with his regiment for this year instead of at once assuming the magnificence of his position in England, in order that he might indulge the spirit of adventure before he assumed the duties of life. And it seemed to him that in dining and sleeping at an Irish priest's house on the shores of the Atlantic, with the prospect of seal shooting and seeing a very pretty girl on the following morning, he was indulging that spirit properly. But Lady Mary Quin thought that he was misbehaving himself and taking to very bad courses. When she heard that he was to sleep at the priest's house, she was quite sure that he would visit Mrs. O'Hara on the next day.

The dinner at the priest's was very jovial. There was a bottle of sherry and there was a bottle of port, procured, chiefly for the sake of appearance, from a grocer's shop at Ennistimon; — but the whiskey had come from Cork and had been in the priest's keeping for the last dozen years. He good-humouredly acknowledged that the wine was nothing, but expressed an opinion that Mr. Neville might find it difficult to beat the "sperrits." "It's thrue for you, Father Marty," said the rival priest from Milltown Malbay, "and it's you that should know good sperrits from bad if ony man in Ireland does."

" 'Deed thin," replied the priest of Liscannor, "barring the famine years, I've mixed two tumblers of punch for meself every day these forty years, and if it was all together it'd be about enough to give Mr. Neville a day's sale-shooting on in his canoe." Immediately after dinner Neville was invited to light his cigar, and everything was easy, comfortable, and to a certain degree adventurous. There were the two priests, and a young Mr. Finucane from Ennistimon, — who however was not quite so much to Fred's taste as the elder men. Mr. Finucane wore various rings, and talked rather largely about his father's demesne. But the whole thing was new, and by no means dull. As Neville had not left Ennis till late in the day, — after what he called a hard day's work in the warrior line, — they did not sit down till past eight o'clock; nor did any one talk of moving till past midnight. Fred certainly made for himself more than two glasses of punch, and he would have sworn that the priest had done so also. Father Marty, however, was said by those who knew him best to be very rigid in this matter, and to have the faculty of making his drink go a long way. Young Mr. Finucane took three or four, — perhaps five or six, — and then volunteered to join Fred Neville in a day's shooting under the rocks. But Fred had not been four years in a cavalry regiment without knowing how to protect himself in such a difficulty as this. "The canoe will only hold myself and the man," said Fred, with perfect simplicity. Mr. Finucane drew himself up haughtily and did not utter another word for the next five minutes. Nevertheless he took a most affectionate leave of the young officer when half an hour after midnight he was told by Father Marty that it was time for him to go home. Father Creech also took his leave, and then Fred and the priest of Liscannor were left sitting together over the embers of the turf fire. "You'll be going up to see our friends at Ardkill to-morrow," said the priest.

"Likely enough, Father Marty."

"In course you will. Sorrow a doubt of that." Then the priest paused.

"And why shouldn't I?" asked Neville.

"I'm not saying that you shouldn't, Mr. Neville. It wouldn't be civil nor yet nathural after knowing them as you have done. If you didn't go they'd be thinking there was a rason for your staying away, and that'd be worse than all. But, Mr. Neville —"

"Out with it, Father Marty." Fred knew what was coming fairly well, and he also had thought a good deal upon the matter.

"Them two ladies, Mr. Neville, live up there all alone, with sorrow a human being in the world to protect them, — barring myself."

"Why should they want protection?"

91

"Just because they're lone women, and because one of them is very young and very beautiful."

"They are both beautiful," said Neville.

" 'Deed and they are, — both of 'em. The mother can look afther herself, and after a fashion, too, she can look afther her daughter. I shouldn't like to be the man to come in her way when he'd once decaived her child. You're a young man, Mr. Neville."

"That's my misfortune."

"And one who stands very high in the world. They tell me you're to be a great lord some day."

"Either that or a little one," said Neville, laughing.

"Anyways you'll be a rich man with a handle to your name. To me, living here in this out of the way parish, a lord doesn't matter that." And Father Marty gave a fillip with his fingers. "The only lord that matters me is me bishop. But with them women yonder, the title and the money and all the grandeur goes a long way. It has been so since the world began. In riding a race against you they carry weight from the very awe which the name of an English Earl brings with it."

"Why should they ride a race against me?"

"Why indeed, — unless you ride a race against them! You wouldn't wish to injure that young thing as isn't yet out of her teens?"

"God forbid that I should injure her."

"I don't think that you're the man to do it with your eyes open, Mr. Neville. If you can't spake her fair in the way of making her your wife, don't spake her fair at all. That's the long and the short of it, Mr. Neville. You see what they are. They're ladies, if there is a lady living in the Queen's dominions. That young thing is as beautiful as Habe, as innocent as a sleeping child, as soft as wax to take impression. What armour has she got against such a one as you?"

"She shall not need armour."

"If you're a gentleman, Mr. Neville, — as I know you are, — you will not give her occasion to find out her own wakeness. Well, if it isn't past one I'm a sinner. It's Friday morning and I mus'n't ate a morsel myself, poor papist that I am; but I'll get you a bit of cold mate and a drop of grog in a moment if you'll take it." Neville, however, refused the hospitable offer.

"Father Marty," he said, speaking with a zeal which perhaps owed something of its warmth to the punch, "you shall find that I am a gentleman."

"I'm shure of it, my boy."

"If I can do no good to your friend, at any rate I will do no harm to her."

"That is spoken like a Christian, Mr. Neville, — which I take to be a higher name even than gentleman."

"There's my hand upon it," said Fred, enthusiastically. After that he went to bed.

On the following morning the priest was very jolly at breakfast, and in speaking of the ladies at Ardkill made no allusion whatever to the conversation of the previous evening. "Ah no," he said, when Neville proposed that they should walk up together to the cottage before he went down to his boat. "What's the good of an ould man like me going bothering? And, signs on, I'm going into Ennistimon to see Pat O'Leary about the milk he's sending to our Union. The thief of the world, — it's wathering it he is before he sends it. Nothing kills me, Mr. Neville, but when I hear of all them English vices being brought over to this poor suffering innocent counthry."

Neville had decided on the advice of Barney Morony, that he would on this morning go down southward along the coast to Drumdeirg rock, in the direction away from the Hag's Head and from Mrs. O'Hara's cottage; and he therefore postponed his expedition till after his visit. When Father Marty started to Ennistimon to look after that sinner O'Leary, Fred Neville, all alone, turned the other way to Ardkill.

Chapter VIII.
I Didn't Want You
to Go.

Mrs. O'Hara had known that he would come, and Kate had known it; and, though it would be unfair to say that they were waiting for him, it is no more than true to say that they were ready for him. "We are so glad to see you again," said Mrs. O'Hara.

"Not more glad than I am to find myself here once more."

"So you dined and slept at Father Marty's last night. What will the grand people say at the Castle?"

"As I sha'n't hear what they say, it won't matter much! Life is not long enough, Mrs. O'Hara, for putting up with disagreeable people."

"Was it pleasant last night?"

"Very pleasant. I don't think Father Creech is half as good as Father Marty, you know."

"Oh no," exclaimed Kate.

"But he's a jolly sort of fellow, too. And there was a Mr. Finucane there, — a very grand fellow."

"We know no one about here but the priests," said Mrs. O'Hara, laughing. "Anybody might think that the cottage was a little convent."

"Then I oughtn't to come."

"Well, no, I suppose not. Only foreigners are admitted to see convents sometimes. You're going after the poor seals again?"

"Barney says the tide is too high for the seals now. We're going to Drumdeirg."

"What, — to those little rocks?" asked Kate.

"Yes, — to the rocks. I wish you'd both come with me."

"I wouldn't go in one of those canoes all out there for the world," said Kate.

"What can be the use of it?" asked Mrs. O'Hara.

"I've got to get the feathers for Father Marty's bed, you know. I haven't shot as many yet as would make a pillow for a cradle."

"The poor innocent gulls!"

"The poor innocent chickens and ducks, if you come to that, Miss O'Hara."

"But they're of use."

"And so will Father Marty's feather bed be of use. Good-bye, Mrs. O'Hara. Good-bye, Miss O'Hara. I shall be down again next week, and we'll have that other seal."

There was nothing in this. So far, at any rate, he had not broken his word to the priest. He had not spoken a word to Kate O'Hara that might not and would not have been said had the priest been present. But how lovely she was; and what a thrill ran through his arm as he held her hand in his for a moment. Where should he find

96

a girl like that in England with such colour, such eyes, such hair, such innocence, — and then with so sweet a voice?

As he hurried down the hill to the beach at Coolroone, where Morony was to meet him with the boat, he could not keep himself from comparisons between Kate O'Hara and Sophie Mellerby. No doubt his comparisons were made very incorrectly, — and unfairly; but they were all in favour of the girl who lived out of the world in solitude on the cliffs of Moher. And why should he not be free to seek a wife where he pleased? In such an affair as that, — an affair of love in which the heart and the heart alone should be consulted, what right could any man have to dictate to him? Certain ideas occurred to him which his friends in England would have called wild, democratic, revolutionary and damnable, but which, owing perhaps to the Irish air and the Irish whiskey and the spirit of adventure fostered by the vicinity of rocks and ocean, appeared to him at the moment to be not only charming but reasonable also. No doubt he was born to high state and great rank, but nothing that his rank and state could give him was so sweet as his liberty. To be free to choose for himself in all things, was the highest privilege of man. What pleasure could he have in a love which should be selected for him by such a woman as his aunt? Then he gave the reins to some confused notion of an Irish bride, a wife who should be half a wife and half not, — whom he would love and cherish tenderly but of whose existence no English friend should be aware. How could he more charmingly indulge his spirit of adventure than by some such arrangement as this?

He knew that he had given a pledge to his uncle to contract no marriage that would be derogatory to his position. He knew also that he had given a pledge to the priest that he would do no harm to Kate O'Hara. He felt that he was bound to keep each pledge. As for that sweet, darling girl, would he not sooner lose his life than harm her? But he was aware that an adventurous life was always a life of difficulties, and that for such as live adventurous lives the duty of overcoming difficulties was of all duties the chief. Then he got into his canoe, and, having succeeded in killing two gulls on the Drumdeirg rocks, thought that for that day he had carried out his purpose as a man of adventure very well.

During February and March he was often on the coast, and hardly one visit did he make which was not followed by a letter from Castle Quin to Scroope Manor. No direct accusation of any special fault was made against him in consequence. No charge was brought of an improper hankering after any special female, because Lady Scroope found herself bound in conscience not to commit her correspondent; but very heavy injunctions were laid upon him as to his general conduct, and he was eagerly entreated to remember his great duty and to come home and settle himself in England. In the mean time the ties which bound him to the coast of Clare were becoming stronger and stronger every day. He had ceased now to care much about seeing Father Marty, and would come, when the tide was low, direct from La-hinch to the strand beneath the cliffs, from whence there was a path through the rocks up to Ardkill. And there he would remain for hours, — having his gun with him, but caring little for his gun. He told himself that he loved the rocks and the wildness of the scenery, and the noise of the ocean, and the whirring of the birds above and below him. It was certainly true that he loved Kate O'Hara.

"Neville, you must answer me a question," said the mother to him one morning when they were out together, looking down upon the Atlantic when the wind had lulled after a gale.

"Ask it then," said he.

"What is the meaning of all this? What is Kate to believe?"

"Of course she believes that I love her better than all the world besides, — that she is more to me than all the world can give or take. I have told her at least, so often, that if she does not believe it she is little better than a Jew."

"You must not joke with me now. If you knew what it was to have one child and only that you would not joke with me."

"I am quite in earnest. I am not joking."

"And what is to be the end of it?"

"The end of it! How can I say? My uncle is an old man, — very old, very infirm, very good, very prejudiced, and broken-hearted because his own son, who died, married against his will."

"You would not liken my Kate to such as that woman was?"

"Your Kate! She is my Kate as much as yours. Such a thought as that would be an injury to me as deep as to you. You know that to me my Kate, our Kate, is all excellence, — as pure and good as she is bright and beautiful. As God is above us she shall be my wife, — but I cannot take her to Scroope Manor as my wife while my uncle lives."

"Why should any one be ashamed of her at Scroope Manor?"

"Because they are fools. But I cannot cure them of their folly. My uncle thinks that I should marry one of my own class."

"Class; — what class? He is a gentleman, I presume, and she is a lady."

"That is very true; — so true that I myself shall act upon the truth. But I will not make his last years wretched. He is a Protestant, and you are Catholics."

"What is that? Are not ever so many of your lords Catholics? Were they not all Catholics before Protestants were ever thought of?"

"Mrs. O'Hara, I have told you that to me she is as high and good and noble as though she were a Princess. And I have told you that she shall be my wife. If that does not content you, I cannot help it. It contents her. I owe much to her."

"Indeed you do; — everything."

"But I owe much to him also. I do not think that you can gain anything by quarrelling with me."

She paused for a while before she answered him, looking into his face the while with something of the ferocity of a tigress. So intent was her gaze that his eyes quailed beneath it. "By the living God," she said, "if you injure my child I will have the very blood from your heart."

Nevertheless she allowed him to return alone to the house, where she knew that he would find her girl. "Kate," he said, going into the parlour in which she was sitting idle at the window, — "dear Kate."

"Well, sir?"

"I'm off."

"You are always — off, as you call it."

"Well, — yes. But I'm not on and off, as the saying is."

"Why should you go away now?"

"Do you suppose a soldier has got nothing to do? You never calculate, I think, that Ennis is about three-and-twenty miles from here. Come, Kate, be nice with me before I go."

"How can I be nice when you are going? I always think when I see you go that you will never come back to me again. I don't know why you should come back to such a place as this?"

"Because, as it happens, the place holds what I love best in all the world." Then he lifted her from her chair, and put his arm round her waist. "Do you not know that I love you better than all that the world holds?"

"How can I know it?"

"Because I swear it to you."

"I think that you like me — a little. Oh Fred, if you were to go and never to come back I should die. Do you remember Mariana? 'My life is dreary. He cometh not,' she said. She said, 'I am aweary, aweary; I would that I were dead!' Do you remember that? What has mother been saying to you?"

"She has been bidding me to do you no harm. It was not necessary. I would sooner pluck out my eye than hurt you. My uncle is an old man, — a very old man. She cannot understand that it is better that we should wait, than that I should have to think hereafter that I had killed him by my unkindness."

"But he wants you to love some other girl."

"He cannot make me do that. All the world cannot change my heart, Kate. If you can not trust me for that, then you do not love me as I love you."

"Oh, Fred, you know I love you. I do trust you. Of course I can wait, if I only know that you will come back to me. I only want to see you." He was now leaning over her, and her cheek was pressed close to his. Though she was talking of Mariana, and pretending to fear future

102

misery, all this was Elysium to her, — the very joy of Paradise. She could sit and think of him now from morning to night, and never find the day an hour too long. She could remember the words in which he made his oaths to her, and cherish the sweet feeling of his arm round her body. To have her cheek close to his was godlike. And then when he would kiss her, though she would rebuke him, it was as though all heaven were in the embrace.

"And now good-bye. One kiss, darling."

"No."

"Not a kiss when I am going?"

"I don't want you to go. Oh, Fred! Well; — there. Good-bye, my own, own, own beloved one. You'll be here on Monday?"

"Yes, — on Monday."

"And be in the boat four hours, and here four minutes. Don't I know you?" But he went without answering this last accusation.

"What shall we do, Kate, if he deceives us?" said the mother that evening.

"Die. But I am sure he will not deceive us."

Neville, as he made his way down to Liscannor, where his gig was waiting for him, did ask himself some serious questions about his adventure. What must be the end of it? And had he not been imprudent? It may be declared on his behalf that no idea of treachery to the girl ever crossed his mind. He loved her too thoroughly for that. He did love her — not perhaps as she loved him. He had many things in the world to

103

occupy his mind, and she had but one. He was almost a god to her. She to him was simply the sweetest girl that he had ever as yet seen, and one who had that peculiar merit that she was all his own. No other man had ever pressed her hand, or drank her sweet breath. Was not such a love a thousand times sweeter than that of some girl who had been hurried from drawing-room to drawing-room, and perhaps from one vow of constancy to another for half-a-dozen years? The adventure was very sweet. But how was it to end? His uncle might live these ten years, and he had not the heart, — nor yet the courage, — to present her to his uncle as his bride.

When he reached Ennis that evening there was a despatch marked "Immediate," from his aunt Lady Scroope. "Your uncle is very ill; — dangerously ill, we fear. His great desire is to see you once again. Pray come without losing an hour."

Early on the following morning he started for Dublin, but before he went to bed that night he not only wrote to Kate O'Hara, but enclosed the note from his aunt. He could understand that though the tidings of his uncle's danger was a shock to him there would be something in the tidings which would cause joy to the two inmates of Ardkill Cottage. When he sent that letter with his own, he was of course determined that he would marry Kate O'Hara as soon as he was a free man.

CHAPTER IX.
FRED NEVILLE
RETURNS TO
SCROOPE.

The suddenness of the demand made for the heir's presence at Scroope was perhaps not owing to the Earl's illness alone. The Earl, indeed, was ill, — so ill that he thought himself that his end was very near; but his illness had been brought about chiefly by the misery to which he had been subjected by the last despatch from Castle Quin to the Countess. "I am most unwilling," she said, "to make mischief or to give unnecessary pain to you or to Lord Scroope; but I think it my duty to let you know that the general opinion about here is that Mr. Neville shall make Miss O'Hara his wife, — *if he has not done so already.* The most dangerous feature in the whole matter is that it is all managed by the priest of this parish, a most unscrupulous person, who would do anything, — he is so daring. We have known him many many years, and we know to what lengths he would go. The laws have been so altered in favour of the Roman Catholics, and against the Protestants, that a priest can do almost just what he likes. I do not think that he would scruple for an instant to marry them if he thought it likely that his prey would escape from him. My own opinion is that there has been no marriage as yet, though I know that others think that there has been." The expression of this opinion from "others" which had reached Lady Mary's ears consisted of an assurance from her own Protestant lady's maid that that wicked, guzzling old Father Marty would marry the young couple as soon as look at them, and very likely had done so already. "I cannot say," continued Lady Mary, "that I actually know anything against the character of Miss O'Hara. Of the mother we have very strange stories here. They live in a little cottage with one maid-servant, almost upon the cliffs, and nobody knows anything about them except the priest. If he should be seduced into a marriage, nothing could be more unfortunate." Lady Mary prob-ably intended to insinuate that were young Neville prudently to get out of the adventure, simply leaving the girl behind him blasted, ruined, and destroyed, the matter no doubt would be bad; but in that case the great misfor-tune would have been avoided. She could not quite say this in plain words; but she felt, no doubt, that Lady Scroope would understand her. Then Lady Mary went on to assure her friend that though she and her father and sisters very greatly regretted that Mr. Neville had not again given them the pleasure of seeing him at Castle Quin, no feeling of injury on that score had induced her to write so strongly as she had done.

She had been prompted to do so simply by her desire to prevent *a most ruinous alliance.*

Lady Scroope acknowledged entirely the truth of these last words. Such an alliance would be most ruinous! But what could she do? Were she to write to Fred and tell him all that she heard, — throwing to the winds Lady Mary's stupid injunctions respecting secrecy, as she would not have scrupled to do could she have thus obtained her object, — might it not be quite possible that she would precipitate the calamity which she desired so eagerly to avoid? Neither had she nor had her husband any power over the young man, except such as arose from his own good feeling. The Earl could not disinherit him; — could not put a single acre beyond his reach. Let him marry whom he might he must be Earl Scroope of Scroope, and the woman so married must be the Countess of Scroope. There was already a Lady Neville about the world whose existence was a torture to them; and if this young man chose also to marry a creature utterly beneath him and to degrade the family, no effort on their part could prevent him. But if, as seemed probable, he were yet free, and if he could be got to come again among them, it might be that he still had left some feelings on which they might work. No doubt there was the Neville obstinacy about him; but he had seemed to both of them to acknowledge the sanctity of his family, and to appreciate in some degree the duty which he owed to it.

The emergency was so great that she feared to act alone. She told everything to her husband, shewing him Lady Mary's letter, and the effect upon him was so great that it made him ill. "It will be better for me," he said, "to turn my face to the wall and die before I know it." He took to his bed, and they of his household did think that he would die. He hardly spoke except to his wife, and when alone with her did not cease to moan over the destruction which had come upon the house. "If it could only have been the other brother," said Lady Scroope.

"There can be no change," said the Earl. "He must do as it lists him with the fortune and the name and the honours of the family."

Then on one morning there was a worse bulletin than heretofore given by the doctor, and Lady Scroope at once sent off the letter which was to recall the nephew to his uncle's bedside. The letter, as we have seen, was successful, and Fred, who caused himself to be carried over from Dorchester to Scroope as fast as post-horses could be made to gallop, almost expected to be told on his arrival that his uncle had departed to his rest. In the hall he encountered Mrs. Bunce the housekeeper. "We think my lord is a little better," said Mrs. Bunce almost in a whisper. "My lord took a little broth in the middle of the day, and we believe he has slept since." Then he passed on and found his aunt in the small sitting-room. His uncle had rallied a little, she told him. She was very affectionate in her manner, and thanked him warmly for his alacrity in coming. When he was told that his uncle would postpone his visit till the next morning he almost began to think that he had been fussy in travelling so quickly.

That evening he dined alone with his aunt, and the conversation during dinner and as they sat for a few minutes after dinner had reference solely to his uncle's health. But, though they were alone on this evening, he was surprised to find that Sophie Mellerby was again at Scroope. Lady Sophia and Mr. Mellerby were up in London, but Sophie was not to join them till May. As it happened, however, she was dining at the parsonage this evening. She must have been in the house when Neville arrived, but he had not seen her. "Is she going to live here?" he asked, almost irreverently, when he was first told that she was in the house. "I wish she were," said Lady Scroope. "I am childless, and she is as dear to me as a daughter." Then Fred apologized, and expressed himself as quite willing that Sophie Mellerby should live and die at Scroope.

The evening was dreadfully dull. It had seemed to him that the house was darker, and gloomier, and more comfortless than ever. He had hurried over to see a dying man, and now there was nothing for him to do but to kick his heels. But before he went to bed his ennui was dissipated by a full explanation of all his aunt's terrors. She crept down to him at about nine, and having commenced her story by saying that she had a matter of most vital importance on which to speak to him, she told him in fact all that she had heard from Lady Mary.

"She is a mischief-making gossiping old maid," said Neville angrily.

"Will you tell me that there is no truth in what she writes?" asked Lady Scroope. But this was a question which Fred Neville was not prepared to answer, and he sat silent. "Fred, tell me the truth. Are you married?"

"No; — I am not married."

"I know that you will not condescend to an untruth."

"If so, my word must be sufficient."

But it was not sufficient. She longed to extract from him some repeated and prolonged assurance which might bring satisfaction to her own mind. "I am glad, at any rate, to hear that there is no truth in that suspicion." To this he would not condescend to reply, but sat glowering at her as though in wrath that any question should be asked him about his private concerns. "You must feel, Fred, for your uncle in such a matter. You must know how important this is to him. You have heard what he has already suffered; and you must know too that he has endeavoured to be very good to you."

"I do know that he has, — been very good to me."

"Perhaps you are angry with me for interfering." He would not deny that he was angry. "I should not do so were it not that your uncle is

110

ill and suffering."

"You have asked me a question and I have answered it. I do not know what more you want of me."

"Will you say that there is no truth in all this that Lady Mary says?"

"Lady Mary is an impertinent old maid."

"If you were in your uncle's place, and if you had an heir as to whose character in the world you were anxious, you would not think anyone impertinent who endeavoured for the sake of friendship to save your name and family from a disreputable connexion."

"I have made no disreputable connexion. I will not allow the word disreputable to be used in regard to any of my friends."

"You do know people of the name of O'Hara?"

"Of course I do."

"And there is a — young lady?"

"I may know a dozen young ladies as to whom I shall not choose to consult Lady Mary Quin."

"You understand what I mean, Fred. Of course I do not wish to ask you anything about your general acquaintances. No doubt you meet many girls whom you admire, and I should be very foolish were I to make inquiries of you or of anybody else concerning them. I am the last person to be so injudicious. If you will tell me that there is not and never shall be any question of marriage between you and Miss O'Hara, I will not say another word."

"I will not pledge myself to anything for the future."

"You told your uncle you would never make a marriage that should be disgraceful to the position which you will be called upon to fill."

"Nor will I."

"But would not this marriage be disgraceful, even were the young lady ever so estimable? How are the old families of the country to be kept up, and the old blood maintained if young men, such as you are, will not remember something of all that is due to the name which they bear."

"I do not know that I have forgotten anything."

Then she paused before she could summon courage to ask him another question. "You have made no promise of marriage to Miss O'Hara?" He sat dumb, but still looking at her with that angry frown. "Surely your uncle has a right to expect that you will answer that question."

"I am quite sure that for his sake it will be much better that no such questions shall be asked me."

In point of fact he had answered the question. When he would not deny that such promise had been made, there could no longer be any doubt of the truth of what Lady Mary had written. Of course the whole truth had now been elicited. He was not married but he was engaged; — engaged to a girl of whom he knew nothing, a Roman Catholic, Irish, fatherless, almost nameless, — to one who had never been seen in good society, one of whom no description could be given, of whom no record could be made in the peerage that would not be altogether disgraceful, a girl of whom he was ashamed to speak before those to whom he owed duty and submission!

That there might be a way to escape the evil even yet Lady Scroope acknowledged to herself fully. Many men promise marriage but do not keep the promise they have made. This lady, who herself was really good, — unselfish, affectionate, religious, actuated by a sense of duty in all that she did, whose life had been almost austerely moral, entertained an idea that young men, such as Fred Neville, very commonly made such promises with very little thought of keeping them. She did not expect young men to be governed by principles such as those to which young ladies are bound to submit themselves. She almost supposed that heaven had a different code of laws for men and women in her condition of life, and that salvation was offered on very different terms to the two sexes. The breach of any such promise as the heir of Scroope could have made to such a girl as this Miss O'Hara would be a perjury at which Jove might certainly be expected to laugh. But in her catalogue there were sins for which no young men could hope to be forgiven; and the sin of such a marriage as this would certainly be beyond pardon.

Of the injury which was to be done to Miss O'Hara, it may be said with certainty that she thought not at all. In her eyes it would be no injury, but simple justice, — no more than a proper punishment for intrigue and wicked ambition. Without having seen the enemy to the family of Scroope, or even having heard a word to her disparagement, she could feel sure that the girl was bad, — that these O'Haras were vulgar and false impostors, persons against whom she could put out all her strength without any prick of conscience. Women in such matters are always hard against women, and especially hard against those whom they believe to belong to a class below their own. Certainly no feeling of mercy would induce her to hold her hand in this task of saving her husband's nephew from an ill-assorted marriage. Mercy to Miss O'Hara! Lady Scroope had the name of being a very charitable woman. She gave away money. She visited the poor. She had laboured hard to make the cottages on the estate clean and comfortable. She denied herself many things that she might give to others. But she would have no more mercy on such a one as Miss O'Hara, than a farmer's labourer would have on a rat!

There was nothing more now to be said to the heir; — nothing more for the present that could serve the purpose which she had in hand. "Your uncle is very ill," she murmured.

"I was so sorry to hear it."

"We hope now that he may recover. For the last two days the doctor has told us that we may hope."

"I am so glad to find that it is so."

"I am sure you are. You will see him to-morrow after breakfast. He is most anxious to see you. I think sometimes you hardly reflect how much you are to him."

"I don't know why you should say so."

"You had better not speak to him to-morrow about this affair, — of the Irish young lady."

"Certainly not, — unless he speaks to me about it."

"He is hardly strong enough yet. But no doubt he will do so before you leave us. I hope it may be long before you do that."

"It can't be very long, Aunt Mary." To this she said nothing, but bade him good-night and he was left alone. It was now past ten, and he supposed that Miss Mellerby had come in and gone to her room. Why she should avoid him in this way he could not understand. But as for Miss Mellerby herself, she was so little to him that he cared not at all whether he did or did not see her. All his brightest thoughts were away in County Clare, on the cliffs overlooking the Atlantic. They might say what they liked to him, but he would never be untrue to the girl whom he had left there. His aunt had spoken of the "affair of — the Irish young lady;" and he had quite understood the sneer with which she had mentioned Kate's nationality. Why should not an Irish girl be as good as any English girl? Of one thing he was quite sure, — that there was much more of real life to be found on the cliffs of Moher than in the gloomy chambers of Scroope Manor.

He got up from his seat feeling absolutely at a loss how to employ himself. Of course he could go to bed, but how terribly dull must life be in a place in which he was obliged to go to bed at ten o'clock because there was nothing to do. And since he had been there his only occupation had been that of listening to his aunt's sermons. He began to think that a man might pay too dearly even for being the heir to Scroope. After sitting awhile in the dark gloom created by a pair of candles, he got up and wandered into the large unused dining-room of the mansion. It was a chamber over forty feet long, with dark flock paper and dark curtains, with dark painted wainscoating below the paper, and huge dark mahogany furniture. On the walls hung the portraits of the Scroopes for many generations past, some in armour, some in their robes of state, ladies with stiff bodices and high head-dresses, not beauties by Lely or warriors and statesmen by Kneller, but wooden, stiff, ungainly, hideous figures, by artists whose works had, unfortunately, been more enduring than their names. He was pacing up and down the room with a candle in his hand, trying to realize to himself what life at Scroope might be with a wife of his aunt's choosing, and his aunt to keep the house for them, when a door was opened at the end of the room, away from that by which he had entered, and with a soft noiseless step

Miss Mellerby entered. She did not see him at first, as the light of her own candle was in her eyes, and she was startled when he spoke to her. His first idea was one of surprise that she should be wandering about the house alone at night. "Oh, Mr. Neville," she said, "you quite took me by surprise. How do you do? I did not expect to meet you here."

"Nor I you!"

"Since Lord Scroope has been so ill, Lady Scroope has been sleeping in the little room next to his, downstairs, and I have just come from her."

"What do you think of my uncle's state?"

"He is better; but he is very weak."

"You see him?"

"Oh yes, daily. He is so anxious to see you, Mr. Neville, and so much obliged to you for coming. I was sure that you would come."

"Of course I came."

"He wanted to see you this afternoon; but the doctor had expressly ordered that he should be kept quiet. Good-night. I am so very glad that you are here. I am sure that you will be good to him."

Why should she be glad, and why should she be sure that he would be good to his uncle? Could it be that she also had been told the story of Kate O'Hara? Then, as no other occupation was possible to him, he took himself to bed.

CHAPTER X.
FRED NEVILLE'S
SCHEME.

On the next morning after breakfast Neville was taken into his uncle's chamber, but there was an understanding that there was to be no conversation on disagreeable subjects on this occasion. His aunt remained in the room while he was there, and the conversation was almost confined to the expression of thanks on the part of the Earl to his nephew for coming, and of hopes on the part of the nephew that his uncle might soon be well. One matter was mooted as to which no doubt much would be said before Neville could get away. "I thought it better to make arrangements to stay a fortnight," said Fred, — as though a fortnight were a very long time indeed.

"A fortnight!" said the Earl.

"We won't talk of his going yet," replied Lady Scroope.

"Supposing I had died, he could not have gone back in a fortnight," said the Earl in a low moaning voice.

"My dear uncle, I hope that I may live to see you in your own place here at Scroope for many years to come." The Earl shook his head, but nothing more was then said on that subject. Fred, however, had carried out his purpose. He had been determined to let them understand that he would not hold himself bound to remain long at Scroope Manor.

Then he wrote a letter to his own Kate. It was the first time he had addressed her in this fashion, and though he was somewhat of a gallant gay Lothario, the writing of the letter was an excitement to him. If so, what must the receipt of it have been to Kate O'Hara! He had promised her that he would write to her, and from the moment that he was gone she was anxious to send in to the post-office at Ennistimon for the treasure which the mail car might bring to her. When she did get it, it was indeed a treasure. To a girl who really loves, the first love letter is a thing as holy as the recollection of the first kiss. "May I see it, Kate?" said Mrs. O'Hara, as her daughter sat poring over the scrap of paper by the window.

"Yes, mamma, — if you please." Then she paused a moment. "But I think that I had rather you did not. Perhaps he did not mean me to shew it." The mother did not urge her request, but contented herself with coming up behind her child and kissing her. The reader, however, shall have the privilege which was denied to Mrs. O'Hara.

DEAREST KATE,
    I got here all alive yesterday at four. I came

119

on as fast as ever I could travel, and hardly got a mouthful to eat after I left Limerick. I never saw such beastliness as they have at the stations. My uncle is much better, — so much so that I shan't remain here very long. I can't tell you any particular news, — except this, that that old cat down at Castle Quin, — the one with the crisp-curled wig, — must have the nose of a dog and the ears of a cat and the eyes of a bird, and she sends word to Scroope of everything that she smells and hears and sees. It makes not the slightest difference to me, — nor to you I should think. Only I hate such interference. The truth is old maids have nothing else to do. If I were you I wouldn't be an old maid.

I can't quite say how long it will be before I am back at Ardkill, but not a day longer than I can help. Address to Scroope, Dorsetshire, — that will be enough; — to F. Neville, Esq. Give my love to your mother. — As for yourself, dear Kate, if you care for my love, you may weigh mine for your own dear self with your own weights and measures. Indeed you have all my heart.

Your own F. N.

There is a young lady here whom it is intended that I shall marry. She is the pink of propriety and really very pretty; — but you need not be a bit jealous. The joke is that my brother is furiously in love with her, and that

I fancy she would be just as much in love with him only that she's told not to. — A thousand kisses.

It was not much of a love letter, but there were a few words in it which sufficed altogether for Kate's happiness. She was told that she had all his heart, — and she believed it. She was told that she need not be jealous of the proper young lady, and she believed that too. He sent her a thousand kisses; and she, thinking that he might have kissed the paper, pressed it to her lips. At any rate his hand had rested on it. She would have been quite willing to shew to her mother all these expressions of her lover's love; but she felt that it would not be fair to him to expose his allusions to the "beastliness" at the stations. He might say what he liked to her; but she understood that she was not at liberty to shew to others words which had been addressed to her in the freedom of perfect intimacy.

"Does he say anything of the old man?" asked Mrs. O'Hara.

"He says that his uncle is better."

"Threatened folks live long. Does Neville tell you when he will be back?"

"Not exactly; but he says that he will not stay long. He does not like Scroope at all. I knew that. He always says that, — that —"

"Says what, dear?"

"When we are married he will go away somewhere, — to Italy or Greece or somewhere.

121

Scroope he says is so gloomy."

"And where shall I go?"

"Oh, mother; — you shall be with us, always."

"No, dear, you must not dream of that. When you have him you will not want me."

"Dear mother. I shall want you always."

"He will not want me. We have no right to expect too much from him, Kate. That he shall make you his wife we have a right to expect. If he were false to you —"

"He is not false. Why should you think him false?"

"I do not think it; but if he were — ! Never mind. If he be true to you, I will not burden him. If I can see you happy, Kate, I will bear all the rest." That which she would have to bear would be utter solitude for life. She could look forward and see how black and tedious would be her days; but all that would be nothing to her if her child were lifted up on high.

It was now the beginning of April, which for sportsmen in England is of all seasons the most desperate. Hunting is over. There is literally nothing to shoot. And fishing, — even if there were fishing in England worth a man's time, — has not begun. A gentleman of enterprise driven very hard in this respect used to declare that there was no remedy for April but to go and fly hawks in Holland. Fred Neville could not fly hawks at Scroope, and found that there was nothing for him to do. Miss Mellerby suggested — books. "I like books better than anything," said Fred. "I always have a lot of novels down at our quarters. But a fellow can't be reading all day, and there isn't a novel in the house except Walter Scott's and a lot of old rubbish. By-the-bye have you read 'All Isn't Gold That Glitters?' " Miss Mellerby had not read the tale named. "That's what I call a good novel."

Day passed after day and it seemed as though he was expected to remain at Scroope without any definite purpose, and, worse still, without any fixed limit to his visit. At his aunt's instigation he rode about the property and asked questions as to the tenants. It was all to be his own, and in the course of nature must be his own very soon. There could not but be an interest for him in every cottage and every field. But yet there was present to him all the time a schoolboy feeling that he was doing a task; and the occupation was not pleasant to him because it was a task. The steward was with him as a kind of pedagogue, and continued to instruct him during the whole ride. This man only paid so much a year, and the rent ought to be so much more; but there were circumstances. And "My Lord" had been peculiarly good. This farm was supposed to be the best on the estate, and that other the worst. Oh yes, there were plenty of foxes. "My Lord" had always insisted that the foxes should be preserved. Some of the hunting gentry no doubt had made complaints, but it was a great shame. Foxes had been seen, two or three at a time, the very day after the coverts had been drawn blank. As for game, a head of game could be got up very soon, as there was plenty of corn and the woods were large; but "My Lord" had never cared for game. The farmers all shot the rabbits on their own land. Rents were paid to the day. There was never any mistake about that. Of course the land would require to be re-valued, but "My Lord" wouldn't hear of such a thing being done in his time. The Manor wood wanted thinning very badly. The wood had been a good deal neglected. "My Lord" had never liked to hear the axe going. That was Grumby Green and the boundary of the estate in that direction. The next farm was college property, and was rented five shillings an acre dearer than "My Lord's" land. If Mr. Neville wished it the steward would show him the limit of the estate on the other side to-morrow. No doubt there was a plan of the estate. It was in "My Lord's" own room, and would shew every farm with its acreage and bounds. Fred thought that he would study this plan on the next day instead of riding about with the steward.

He could not escape from the feeling that he was being taught his lesson like a school-boy, and he did not like it. He longed for the freedom of his boat on the Irish coast, and longed for the devotedness of Kate O'Hara. He was sure that he loved her so thoroughly that life without her was not to be regarded as possible. But certain vague ideas very injurious to the Kate he so dearly loved crossed his brain. Under the constant teaching of his aunt he did recognize it as a fact that he owed a high duty to his family. For many days after that first night at Scroope not a word was said to him about Kate O'Hara. He saw his uncle daily, — probably twice a day; but the Earl never alluded to his Irish love. Lady Scroope spoke constantly of the greatness of the position which the heir was called upon to fill and of all that was due to the honour of the family. Fred, as he heard her, would shake his head impatiently, but would acknowledge the truth of what she said. He was induced even to repeat the promise which he had made to his uncle, and to assure his aunt that he would do nothing to mar or lessen the dignity of the name of Neville. He did become, within his own mind, indoctrinated with the idea that he would injure the position of the earldom which was to be his were he to marry Kate O'Hara. Arguments which had appeared to him to be absurd when treated with ridicule by Father Marty, and which in regard to his own conduct he had determined to treat as old women's tales, seemed to him at Scroope to be true and binding. The atmosphere of the place, the companionship of Miss Mellerby, the reverence with which he himself was treated by the domestics, the signs of high nobility which surrounded him on all sides, had their effect upon him. Noblesse oblige. He felt that it was so. Then there crossed his brain visions of a future life which were injurious to the girl he loved.

Let his brother Jack come and live at Scroope and marry Sophie Mellerby. As long as he lived Jack could not be the Earl, but in regard to money he would willingly make such arrangements as would enable his brother to maintain the dignity and state of the house. They would divide the income. And then he would so arrange his matters with Kate O'Hara that his brother's son should be heir to the Earldom. He had some glimmering of an idea that as Kate was a Roman Catholic a marriage ceremony might be contrived of which this would become the necessary result. There should be no deceit. Kate should know it all, and everything should be done to make her happy. He would live abroad, and would not call himself by his title. They would be Mr. and Mrs. Neville. As to the property, that must of course hereafter go with the title, but in giving up so much to his brother, he could of course arrange as to the provision necessary for any children of his own. No doubt his Kate would like to be the Countess Scroope, — would prefer that a future son of her own should be the future Earl. But as he was ready to abandon so much, surely she would be ready to abandon something. He must explain to her, — and to her mother, — that under no other circumstances could he marry her. He must tell her of pledges made to his uncle before he knew her, of the duty which he owed to his family, and of his own great dislike to the kind of life which would await him as acting head of the family. No doubt there would be scenes, — and his heart quailed as he remembered certain glances which had flashed upon him from the eyes of Mrs. O'Hara. But was he not offering to give up everything for his love? His Kate should be his wife after some Roman Catholic fashion in some Roman Catholic country. Of course there would be difficulties, — the least of which would not be those glances from the angry mother; but it would be his business to overcome difficulties. There were always difficulties in the way of any man who chose to leave the common grooves of life and to make a separate way for himself. There were always difficulties in the way of adventures. Dear Kate! He would never desert his Kate. But his Kate must do as much as this for him. Did he not intend that, whatever good things the world might have in store for him, his Kate should share them all?

His ideas were very hazy, and he knew himself that he was ignorant of the laws respecting marriage. It occurred to him, therefore, that he had better consult his brother, and confide everything to him. That Jack was wiser than he, he was always willing to allow; and although he did in some sort look down upon Jack as a plodding fellow, who shot no seals and cared nothing for adventure, still he felt it to be almost a pity that Jack should not be the future Earl. So he told his aunt that he proposed to ask his brother to come to Scroope for a day or two before he returned to Ireland. Had his aunt, or would his

127

uncle have, any objection? Lady Scroope did not dare to object. She by no means wished that her younger nephew should again be brought within the influence of Miss Mellerby's charms; but it would not suit her purpose to give offence to the heir by refusing so reasonable request. He would have been off to join his brother at Woolwich immediately. So the invitation was sent, and Jack Neville promised that he would come.

Fred knew nothing of the offer that had been made to Miss Mellerby, though he had been sharp enough to discern his brother's feelings. "My brother is coming here to-morrow," he said one morning to Miss Mellerby when they were alone together.

"So Lady Scroope has told me. I don't wonder that you should wish to see him."

"I hope everybody will be glad to see him. Jack is just about the very best fellow in the world; — and he's one of the cleverest too."

"It is so nice to hear one brother speak in that way of another."

"I swear by Jack. He ought to have been the elder brother; — that's the truth. Don't you like him?"

"Who; — I. Oh, yes, indeed. What I saw of him I liked very much."

"Isn't it a pity that he shouldn't have been the elder?"

"I can't say that, Mr. Neville."

"No. It wouldn't be just civil to me. But I can say it. When we were here last winter I thought that my brother was —"

"Was what, Mr Neville?"

"Was getting to be very fond of you. Perhaps I ought not to say so."

"I don't think that much good is ever done by saying that kind of thing," said Miss Mellerby gravely.

"It cannot at any rate do any harm in this case. I wish with all my heart that he was fond of you and you of him."

"That is all nonsense. Indeed it is."

"I am not saying it without an object. I don't see why you and I should not understand one another. If I tell you a secret will you keep it?"

"Do not tell me any secret that I must keep from Lady Scroope."

"But that is just what you must do."

"But then suppose I don't do it," said Miss Mellerby.

But Fred was determined to tell his secret. "The truth is that both my uncle and my aunt want me to fall in love with you."

"How very kind of them," said she with a little forced laugh.

"I don't for a moment think that, had I tried it on ever so, I could have succeeded. I am not at all the sort of man to be conceited in that way. Wishing to do the best they could for me, they picked you out. It isn't that I don't think as well of you as they do, but —"

"Really, Mr. Neville, this is the oddest conversation."

"Quite true. It is odd. But the fact is you are here, and there is nobody else I can talk to. And I want you to know the exact truth. I'm engaged to — somebody else."

"I ought to break my heart; — oughtn't I?"

"I don't in the least mind your laughing at me. I should have minded it very much if I had asked you to marry me, and you had refused me."

"You haven't given me the chance, you see."

"I didn't mean. What was the good?"

"Certainly not, Mr. Neville, if you are engaged to some one else. I shouldn't like to be Number Two."

"I'm in a peck of troubles; — that's the truth. I would change places with my brother to-morrow if I could. I daresay you don't believe that, but I would. I will not vex my uncle if I can help it, but I certainly shall not throw over the girl who loves me. If it wasn't for the title, I'd give up Scroope to my brother to-morrow, and go and live in some place where I could get lots of shooting, and where I should never have to put on a white choker."

"You'll think better of all that."

"Well! — I've just told you everything because I like to be on the square. I wish you knew Kate O'Hara. I'm sure you would not wonder that a fellow should love her. I had rather you didn't tell my aunt what I have told you; but if you choose to do so, I can't help it."

CHAPTER XI.
THE WISDOM OF JACK NEVILLE.

Neville had been forced to get his leave of absence renewed on the score of his uncle's health, and had promised to prolong his absence till the end of April. When doing so he had declared his intention of returning to Ennis in the beginning of May; but no agreement to that had as yet been expressed by his uncle or aunt. Towards the end of the month his brother came to Scroope, and up to that time not a word further had been said to him respecting Kate O'Hara.

He had received an answer from Kate to his letter, prepared in a fashion very different from that of his own. He had seated himself at a table and in compliance with the pledge given by him, had scrawled off his epistle as fast as he could write it. She had taken a whole morning to think of hers, and had re-copied it after composing it, and had then read it with the utmost care, confessing to herself, almost with tears, that it was altogether unworthy of him to whom it was to be sent. It was the first love letter she had ever written, — probably the first letter she had ever written to a man, except those short notes which she would occasionally scrawl to Father Marty in compliance with her mother's directions. The letter to Fred was as follows; —

Ardkill Cottage,
10th April, 18—.
MY DEAREST FRED,

I received your dear letter three or four days ago, and it made me so happy. We were sorry that you should have such an uncomfortable journey; but all that would be over and soon forgotten when you found yourself in your comfortable home and among your own friends. I am very glad to hear that your uncle is better. The thought of finding him so ill must have made your journey very sad. As he is so much better, I suppose you will come back soon to your poor little Kate.

There is no news at all to send you from Liscannor. Father Marty was up here yesterday and says that your boat is all safe at Lahinch. He says that Barney Morony is an idle fellow, but as he has nothing to do he can't help being idle. You should come back and not let him be idle any more. I think the sea gulls know that you are away, because they are wheeling and screaming about louder and bolder than ever.

Mother sends her best love. She is very well. We have had nothing to eat since you went because it has been Lent. So, if you had

132

been here, you would not have been able to get a bit of luncheon. I dare say you have been a great deal better off at Scroope. Father Marty says that you Protestants will have to keep your Lent hereafter, — eighty days at a time instead of forty; and that we Catholics will be allowed to eat just what we like, while you Protestants will have to look on at us. If so, I think I'll manage to give you a little bit.

Do come back to your own Kate as soon as you can. I need not tell you that I love you better than all the world because you know it already. I am not a bit jealous of the proper young lady, and I hope that she will fall in love with your brother. Then some day we shall be sisters; — shan't we? I should like to have a proper young lady for my sister so much. Only, perhaps she would despise me. Do come back soon. Everything is so dull while you are away! You would come back to your own Kate if you knew how great a joy it is to her when she sees you coming along the cliff.

Dearest, dearest love, I am always your own,

own
KATE O'HARA.

Neville thought of showing Kate's letter to Miss Mellerby, but when he read it a second time he made up his mind that he would keep it to himself. The letter was all very well, and, as regarded the expressions towards himself, just what it should be. But he felt that it was not such a letter as Miss Mellerby would have written herself, and he was a little ashamed of all that was said about the priest. Neither was he proud of the pretty, finished, French handwriting, over every letter of which his love had taken so much pains. In truth, Kate O'Hara was better educated than himself, and perhaps knew as much as Sophie Mellerby. She could have written her letter quite as well in French as in English, and she did understand something of the formation of her sentences. Fred Neville had been at an excellent school, but it may be doubted whether he could have explained his own written language. Nevertheless he was a little ashamed of his Kate, and thought that Miss Mellerby might perceive her ignorance if he shewed her letter.

He had sent for his brother in order that he might explain his scheme and get his brother's advice; — but he found it very difficult to explain his scheme to Jack Neville. Jack, indeed, from the very first would not allow that the scheme was in any way practicable. "I don't quite understand, Fred, what you mean. You don't intend to deceive her by a false marriage?"

"Most assuredly not. I do not intend to deceive her at all."

"You must make her your wife, or not make her your wife."

"Undoubtedly she will be my wife. I am quite

determined about that. She has my word, — and over and above that, she is dearer to me than anything else."

"If you marry her, her eldest son must of course be the heir to the title."

"I am not at all so sure of that. All manner of queer things may be arranged by marriages with Roman Catholics."

"Put that out of your head," said Jack Neville. "In the first place you would certainly find yourself in a mess, and in the next place the attempt itself would be dishonest. I dare say men have crept out of marriages because they have been illegal; but a man who arranges a marriage with the intention of creeping out of it is a scoundrel."

"You needn't bully about it, Jack. You know very well that I don't mean to creep out of anything."

"I'm sure you don't. But as you ask me I must tell you what I think. You are in a sort of dilemma between this girl and Uncle Scroope."

"I'm not in any dilemma at all."

"You seem to think you have made some promise to him which will be broken if you marry her; — and I suppose you certainly have made her a promise."

"Which I certainly mean to keep," said Fred.

"All right. Then you must break your promise to Uncle Scroope."

"It was a sort of half and half promise. I could not bear to see him making himself unhappy about it."

"Just so. I suppose Miss O'Hara can wait."

Fred Neville scratched his head. "Oh yes; — she can wait. There's nothing to bind me to a day or a month. But my uncle may live for the next ten years now."

"My advice to you is to let Miss O'Hara understand clearly that you will make no other engagement, but that you cannot marry her as long as your uncle lives. Of course I say this on the supposition that the affair cannot be broken off."

"Certainly not," said Fred with a decision that was magnanimous.

"I cannot think the engagement a fortunate one for you in your position. Like should marry like. I'm quite sure of that. You would wish your wife to be easily intimate with the sort of people among whom she would naturally be thrown as Lady Scroope, — among the wives and daughters of other Earls and such like."

"No; I shouldn't."

"I don't see how she would be comfortable in any other way."

"I should never live among other Earls, as you call them. I hate that kind of thing. I hate London. I should never live here."

"What would you do?"

"I should have a yacht, and live chiefly in that. I should go about a good deal, and get into all manner of queer places. I don't say but what I might spend a winter now and then in Leicestershire or Northamptonshire, for I am fond of hunting. But I should have no regular home. According to my scheme you should have this place, — and sufficient of the income to maintain it of course."

"That wouldn't do, Fred," said Jack, shaking his head, — "though I know how generous you are."

"Why wouldn't it do?"

"You are the heir, and you must take the duties with the privileges. You can have your yacht if you like a yacht, — but you'll soon get tired of that kind of life. I take it that a yacht is a bad place for a nursery, and inconvenient for one's old boots. When a man has a home fixed for him by circumstances, — as you will have, — he gravitates towards it, let his own supposed predilections be what they may. Circumstances are stronger than predilections."

"You're a philosopher."

"I was always more sober than you, Fred."

"I wish you had been the elder, — on the condition of the younger brother having a tidy slice out of the property to make himself comfortable."

"But I am not the elder, and you must take the position with all the encumbrances. I see nothing for it but to ask Miss O'Hara to wait. If my uncle lives long the probability is that one or the other of you will change your minds, and that the affair will never come off."

When the younger and wiser brother gave this

advice he did not think it all likely that Miss O'Hara would change her mind. Penniless young ladies don't often change their minds when they are engaged to the heirs of Earls. It was not at all probable that she should repent the bargain that she had made. But Jack Neville did think it very probable that his brother might do so; — and, indeed, felt sure that he would do so if years were allowed to intervene. His residence in County Clare would not be perpetual, and with him in his circumstances it might well be that the young lady, being out of sight, should be out of mind. Jack could not exactly declare his opinion on this head. His brother at present was full of his promise, full of his love, full of his honour. Nor would Jack have absolutely coun-selled him to break his word to the young lady. But he thought it probable that in the event of delay poor Miss O'Hara might go to the wall; — and he also thought that for the general interests of the Scroope family it would be better that she should do so.

"And what are you going to do yourself?" asked Fred.

"In respect of what?"

"In respect of Miss Mellerby?"

"In respect of Miss Mellerby I am not going to do anything," said Jack as he walked away.

In all that the younger brother said to the elder as to poor Kate O'Hara he was no doubt wise and prudent; but in what he said about himself he did not tell the truth. But then the question asked was one which a man is hardly bound to answer, even to a brother. Jack Neville was much less likely to talk about his love affairs than Fred, but not on that account less likely to think about them. Sophie Mellerby had refused him once, but young ladies have been known to marry gentlemen after refusing them more than once. He at any rate was determined to persevere, having in himself and in his affairs that silent faith of which the possessor is so often unconscious, but which so generally leads to success. He found Miss Mellerby to be very courteous to him if not gracious; and he had the advantage of not being afraid of her. It did not strike him that because she was the granddaughter of a duke, and because he was a younger son, that therefore he ought not to dare to look at her. He understood very well that she was brought there that Fred might marry her; — but Fred was intent on marrying some one else, and Sophie Mellerby was not a girl to throw her heart away upon a man who did not want it. He had come to Scroope for only three days, but, in spite of some watchfulness on the part of the Countess, he found his opportunity for speaking before he left the house. "Miss Mellerby," he said, "I don't know whether I ought to thank Fortune or to upbraid her for having again brought me face to face with you."

"I hope the evil is not so oppressive as to make you very loud in your upbraidings."

"They shall not at any rate be heard. I don't

know whether there was any spice of malice about my brother when he asked me to come here, and told me in the same letter that you were at Scroope."

"He must have meant it for malice, I should think," said the young lady, endeavouring, but not quite successfully, to imitate the manner of the man who loved her.

"Of course I came."

"Not on my behalf, I hope, Mr. Neville."

"Altogether on your behalf. Fred's need to see me was not very great, and, as my uncle had not asked me, and as my aunt, I fancy, does not altogether approve of me, I certainly should not have come, — were it not that I might find it difficult to get any other opportunity of seeing you."

"That is hardly fair to Lady Scroope, Mr. Neville."

"Quite fair, I think. I did not come clandestinely. I am not ashamed of what I am doing, — or of what I am going to do. I may be ashamed of this, — that I should feel my chance of success to be so small. When I was here before I asked you to — allow me to love you. I now ask you again."

"Allow you!" she said.

"Yes; — allow me. I should be too bold were I to ask you to return my love at once. I only ask you to know that because I was repulsed once, I have not given up the pursuit."

"Mr. Neville, I am sure that my father and

mother would not permit it."

"May I ask your father, Miss Mellerby?"

"Certainly not, — with my permission."

"Nevertheless you will not forget that I am suitor for your love?"

"I will make no promise of anything, Mr. Neville." Then, fearing that she had encouraged him, she spoke again. "I think you ought to take my answer as final."

"Miss Mellerby, I shall take no answer as final that is not favourable. Should I indeed hear that you were to be married to another man, that would be final; but that I shall not hear from your own lips. You will say good-bye to me," and he offered her his hand.

She gave him her hand; — and he raised it to his lips and kissed it, as men were wont to do in the olden days.

Chapter XII.
Fred Neville
Makes a Promise.

Fred Neville felt that he had not received from his brother the assistance or sympathy which he had required. He had intended to make a very generous offer, — not indeed quite understanding how his offer could be carried out, but still of a nature that should, he thought, have bound his brother to his service. But Jack had simply answered him by sermons; — by sermons and an assurance of the impracticability of his scheme. Nevertheless he was by no means sure that his scheme was impracticable. He was at least sure of this, — that no human power could force him to adopt a mode of life that was distasteful to him. No one could make him marry Sophie Mellerby, or any other Sophie, and maintain a grand and gloomy house in Dorsetshire, spending his income, not in a manner congenial to him, but in keeping a large retinue of servants and taking what he called the "heavy line" of an English nobleman. The property must be his own, — or at any rate the life use of it. He swore to himself over and over again that nothing should induce him to impoverish the family or to leave the general affairs of the house of Scroope worse than he found them. Much less than half of that which he understood to be the income coming from the estates would suffice for him. But let his uncle or aunt, — or his strait-laced methodical brother, say what they would to him, nothing should induce him to make himself a slave to an earldom.

But yet his mind was much confused and his contentment by no means complete. He knew that there must be a disagreeable scene between himself and his uncle before he returned to Ireland, and he knew also that his uncle could, if he were so minded, stop his present very liberal allowance altogether. There had been a bargain, no doubt, that he should remain with his regiment for a year, and of that year six months were still unexpired. His uncle could not quarrel with him for going back to Ireland; but what answer should he make when his uncle asked him whether he were engaged to marry Miss O'Hara, — as of course he would ask; and what reply should he make when his uncle would demand of him whether he thought such a marriage fit for a man in his position. He knew that it was not fit. He believed in the title, in the sanctity of the name, in the mysterious grandeur of the family. He did not think that an Earl of Scroope ought to marry a girl of whom nothing whatever was known. The pride of the position stuck to him; — but it irked him to feel that the sacrifices necessary to support that pride should fall on his own shoulders.

One thing was impossible to him. He would not desert his Kate. But he wished to have his Kate, as a thing apart. If he could have given six months of each year to his Kate, living that yacht-life of which he had spoken, visiting those strange sunny places which his imagination had pictured to him, unshackled by conventionalities, beyond the sound of church bells, unimpeded by any considerations of family, — and then have migrated for the other six months to his earldom and his estates, to his hunting and perhaps to Parliament, leaving his Kate behind him, that would have been perfect. And why not? In the days which must come so soon, he would be his own master. Who could impede his motions or gainsay his will? Then he remembered his Kate's mother, and the glances which would come from the mother's eyes. There might be difficulty even though Scroope were all his own.

He was not a villain; — simply a self-indulgent spoiled young man who had realized to himself no idea of duty in life. He never once told himself that Kate should be his mistress. In all the pictures which he drew for himself of a future life everything was to be done for her happiness and for her gratification. His yacht should be made a floating bower for her delight. During those six months of the year which, and which only, the provoking circumstances of his position would enable him to devote to joy and love, her will should be his law. He did not think himself to be fickle. He would never want another Kate. He would leave her with sorrow. He would return to her with ecstasy. Everybody around him should treat her with the respect due to an empress. But it would be very expedient that she should be called Mrs. Neville instead of Lady Scroope. Could things not be so arranged for him; — so arranged that he might make a promise to his uncle, and yet be true to his Kate without breaking his promise? That was his scheme. Jack said that his scheme was impracticable. But the difficulties in his way were not, he thought, so much those which Jack had propounded as the angry eyes of Kate O'Hara's mother.

At last the day was fixed for his departure. The Earl was already so much better as to be able to leave his bedroom. Twice or thrice a day Fred saw his uncle, and there was much said about the affairs of the estate. The heir had taken some trouble, had visited some of the tenants, and had striven to seem interested in the affairs of the property. The Earl could talk for ever about the estate, every field, every fence, almost every tree on which was familiar to him. That his tenants should be easy in their circumstances, a protestant, church-going, rent-paying people, son following father, and daughters marrying as their mothers had married, unchanging, never sinking an inch in the social scale, or rising, — this was the wish nearest to his heart. Fred was well disposed to talk about the tenants as long as Kate O'Hara was not mentioned. When the Earl would mournfully speak of his own coming death, as an event which could not now be far distant, Fred with fullest sincerity would promise that his wishes should be observed. No rents should be raised. The axe should be but sparingly used. It seemed to him strange that a man going into eternity should care about this tree or that; — but as far as he was concerned the trees should stand while Nature supported them. No servant should be dismissed. The carriage horses should be allowed to die on the place. The old charities should be maintained. The parson of the parish should always be a welcome guest at the Manor. No promise was difficult for him to make so long as that one question were left untouched.

But when he spoke of the day of his departure as fixed, — as being "the day after to-morrow," — then he knew that the question must be touched. "I am sorry, — very sorry, that you must go," said the Earl.

"You see a man can't leave the service at a moment's notice."

"I think that we could have got over that, Fred."

"Perhaps as regards the service we might, but the regiment would think ill of me. You see, so many things depend on a man's staying or going. The youngsters mayn't have their money ready. I said I should remain till October."

"I don't at all wish to act the tyrant to you."

"I know that, uncle."

Then there was a pause. "I haven't spoken to you yet, Fred, on a matter which has caused me a great deal of uneasiness. When you first came I was not strong enough to allude to it, and I left it to your aunt." Neville knew well what was coming now, and was aware that he was moved in a manner that hardly became his manhood. "Your aunt tells me that you have got into some trouble with a young lady in the west of Ireland."

"No trouble, uncle, I hope."

"Who is she?"

Then there was another pause, but he gave a direct answer to the question. "She is a Miss O'Hara."

"A Roman Catholic?"

"Yes."

"A girl of whose family you know nothing?"

"I know that she lives with her mother."

"In absolute obscurity, — and poverty?"

"They are not rich," said Fred.

"Do not suppose that I regard poverty as a fault. It is not necessary that you should marry a girl with any fortune."

"I suppose not, Uncle Scroope."

"But I understand that this young lady is quite beneath yourself in life. She lives with her mother in a little cottage, without servants, —"

"There is a servant."

"You know what I mean, Fred. She does not live as ladies live. She is uneducated."

"You are wrong there, my lord. She has been

147

at an excellent school in France."

"In France! Who was her father, and what?"

"I do not know what her father was; — a Captain O'Hara, I believe."

"And you would marry such a girl as that; — a Roman Catholic; picked up on the Irish coast, — one of whom nobody knows even her parentage or perhaps her real name? It would kill me, Fred."

"I have not said that I mean to marry her."

"But what do you mean? Would you ruin her; — seduce her by false promises and then leave her? Do you tell me that in cold blood you look forward to such a deed as that?"

"Certainly not."

"I hope not, my boy; I hope not that. Do not tell me that a heartless scoundrel is to take my name when I am gone."

"I am not a heartless scoundrel," said Fred Neville, jumping up from his seat.

"Then what is it that you mean? You have thought, have you not, of the duties of the high position to which you are called? You do not suppose that wealth is to be given to you, and a great name, and all the appanages and power of nobility, in order that you may eat more, and drink more, and lie softer than others. It is because some think so, and act upon such base thoughts, that the only hereditary peerage left in the world is in danger of encountering the ill will of the people. Are you willing to be known only as one of those who have disgraced their order?"

"I do not mean to disgrace it."

"But you will disgrace it if you marry such a girl as that. If she were fit to be your wife, would not the family of Lord Kilfenora have known her?"

"I don't think much of their not knowing her, uncle."

"Who does know her? Who can say that she is even what she pretends to be? Did you not promise me that you would make no such marriage?"

He was not strong to defend his Kate. Such defence would have been in opposition to his own ideas, in antagonism with the scheme which he had made for himself. He understood, almost as well as did his uncle, that Kate O'Hara ought not to be made Countess of Scroope. He too thought that were she to be presented to the world as the Countess of Scroope, she would disgrace the title. And yet he would not be a villain! And yet he would not give her up! He could only fall back upon his scheme. "Miss O'Hara is as good as gold," he said; "but I acknowledge that she is not fit to be mistress of this house."

"Fred," said the Earl, almost in a passion of affectionate solicitude, "do not go back to Ireland. We will arrange about the regiment. No harm shall be done to any one. My health will be your excuse, and the lawyers shall arrange it all."

"I must go back," said Neville. Then the Earl fell back in his chair and covered his face with his hands. "I must go back; but I will give you my honour as a gentleman to do nothing that shall distress you."

"You will not marry her?"

"No."

"And, oh, Fred, as you value your own soul, do not injure a poor girl so desolate as that. Tell her and tell her mother the honest truth. If there be tears, will not that be better than sorrow, and disgrace, and ruin?" Among evils there must always be a choice; and the Earl thought that a broken promise was the lightest of those evils to a choice among which his nephew had subjected himself.

And so the interview was over, and there had been no quarrel. Fred Neville had given the Earl a positive promise that he would not marry Kate O'Hara, — to whom he had sworn a thousand times that she should be his wife. Such a promise, however, — so he told himself — is never intended to prevail beyond the lifetime of the person to whom it is made. He had bound himself not to marry Kate O'Hara while his uncle lived, and that was all.

Or might it not be better to take his uncle's advice altogether and tell the truth, — not to Kate, for that he could not do, — but to Mrs. O'Hara or to Father Marty? As he thought of this he acknowledged to himself that the task of telling such a truth to Mrs. O'Hara would be almost beyond his strength. Could he not throw himself upon the priest's charity, and leave it all to him? Then he thought of his own Kate, and some feeling akin to genuine love told him that he could not part with the girl in such fashion as that. He would break his heart were he to lose his Kate. When he looked at it in that light it seemed to him that Kate was more to him than all the family of the Scroopes with all their glory. Dear, sweet, soft, innocent, beautiful Kate! His Kate who, as he knew well, worshipped the very ground on which he trod! It was not possible that he should separate himself from Kate O'Hara.

On his return to Ireland he turned that scheme of his over and over again in his head. Surely something might be done if the priest would stand his friend! What if he were to tell the whole truth to the priest, and ask for such assistance as a priest might give him? But the one assurance to which he came during his journey was this; — that when a man goes in for adventures, he requires a good deal of skill and some courage too to carry him through them.

■ ■ ■ ■

VOLUME II.

■ ■ ■ ■

CHAPTER I.
FROM BAD TO WORSE.

As he was returning to Ennis Neville was so far removed from immediate distress as to be able to look forward without fear to his meeting with the two ladies at Ardkill. He could as yet take his Kate in his arms without any hard load upon his heart, such as would be there if he knew that it was incumbent upon him at once to explain his difficulties. His uncle was still living, but was old and still ill. He would naturally make the most of the old man's age and infirmities. There was every reason why they should wait, and no reason why such waiting should bring reproaches upon his head. On the night of his arrival at his quarters he despatched a note to his Kate.

DEAREST LOVE.

Here I am again in the land of freedom and potatoes. I need not trouble you with writing about home news, as I shall see you the day after to-morrow. All to-morrow and Wednesday morning I must stick close to my guns here. After one on Wednesday I shall be free. I will drive over to Lahinch, and come round in the boat. I must come back here the same night, but I suppose it will be the next morning before I get to bed. I sha'n't mind that if I get something for my pains. My love to your mother. Your own,

F. N.

In accordance with this plan he did drive over to Lahinch. He might have saved time by directing that his boat should come across the bay to meet him at Liscannor, but he felt that he would prefer not to meet Father Marty at present. It might be that before long he would be driven to tell the priest a good deal, and to ask for the priest's assistance; but at present he was not anxious to see Father Marty. Barney Morony was waiting for him at the stable where he put up his horse, and went down with him to the beach. The ladies, according to Barney, were quite well and more winsome than ever. But, — and this information was not given without much delay and great beating about the bush, — there was a rumour about Liscannor that Captain O'Hara had "turned up." Fred was so startled at this that he could not refrain from showing his anxiety by the questions which he asked. Barney did not seem to think that the Captain had been at Ardkill or anywhere in the neighbourhood. At any rate he, Barney, had not seen him. He had just heard the rumour. "Shure, Captain, I wouldn't be telling yer honour a lie; and they do be saying that the Captain one time was as fine a man as a woman ever sot eyes on; — and why not, seeing what kind the young lady is, God bless her!" If it were true that Kate's father had "turned up," such an advent might very naturally alter Neville's plans. It would so change the position of things as to relieve him in some degree from the force of his past promises.

Nevertheless when he saw Kate coming along the cliffs to meet him, the one thing more certain to him than all other things was that he would never abandon her. She had been watching for him almost from the hour at which he had said that he would leave Ennis, and, creeping up among the rocks, had seen his boat as it came round the point from Liscannor. She had first thought that she would climb down the path to meet him; but the tide was high and there was now no strip of strand below the cliffs; and Barney Morony would have been there to see; and she resolved that it would be nicer to wait for him on the summit. "Oh Fred, you have come back," she said, throwing herself on his breast.

"Yes; I am back. Did you think I was going to desert you?"

"No; no. I knew you would not desert me. Oh, my darling!"

"Dear Kate; — dearest Kate."

"You have thought of me sometimes?"

"I have thought of you always, — every hour." And so he swore to her that she was as much to him as he could possibly be to her. She hung on his arm as she went down to the cottage, and believed herself to be the happiest and most fortunate girl in Ireland. As yet no touch of the sorrows of love had fallen upon her.

He could not all at once ask her as to that rumour which Morony had mentioned to him. But he thought of it as he walked with his arm round her waist. Some question must be asked, but it might, perhaps, be better that he should ask it of the mother. Mrs. O'Hara was at the cottage and seemed almost as glad to see him as Kate had been. "It is very pleasant to have you back again," she said. "Kate has been counting first the hours, and then the minutes."

"And so have you, mother."

"Of course we want to hear all the news," said Mrs. O'Hara. Then Neville, with the girl who was to be his wife sitting close beside him on the sofa, — almost within his embrace, — told them how things were going at Scroope. His uncle was very weak, — evidently failing; but still so much better as to justify the heir in coming away. He might perhaps live for another twelve months, but the doctors thought it hardly possible that he should last longer than that. Then the nephew went on to say that his uncle was the best and most generous man in the world, — and the finest gentleman and the truest Christian. He told also of the tenants who were not to be harassed, and the servants who were not to be dismissed, and the horses that were to be allowed to die in their beds, and the trees that were not to be cut down.

"I wish I knew him," said Kate. "I wish I could have seen him once."

"That can never be," said Fred, sadly.

"No; — of course not."

Then Mrs. O'Hara asked a question. "Has he ever heard of us?"

"Yes; — he has heard of you."

"From you?"

"No; — not first from me. There are many reasons why I would not have mentioned your names could I have helped it. He has wished me to marry another girl, — and especially a Protestant girl. That was impossible."

"That must be impossible now, Fred," said Kate, looking up into his face.

"Quite so, dearest; but why should I have vexed him, seeing that he is so good to me, and that he must be gone so soon?"

"Who had told him of us?" asked Mrs. O'Hara.

"That woman down there at Castle Quin."

"Lady Mary?"

"Foul-tongued old maid that she is," exclaimed Fred. "She writes to my aunt by every post, I believe."

"What evil can she say of us?"

"She does say evil. Never mind what. Such a woman always says evil of those of her sex who are good-looking."

"There, mother; — that's for you," said Kate, laughing. "I don't care what she says."

"If she tells your aunt that we live in a small cottage, without servants, without society, with

159

just the bare necessaries of life, she tells the truth of us."

"That's just what she does say; — and she goes on harping about religion. Never mind her. You can understand that my uncle should be old-fashioned. He is very old, and we must wait."

"Waiting is so weary," said Mrs. O'Hara.

"It is not weary for me at all," said Kate.

Then he left them, without having said a word about the Captain. He found the Captain to be a subject very uncomfortable to mention, and thought as he was sitting there that it might perhaps be better to make his first enquiries of this priest. No one said a word to him about the Captain beyond what he had heard from his boatman. For, as it happened, he did not see the priest till May was nearly past, and during all that time things were going from bad to worse. As regarded any services which he rendered to the army at this period of his career, the excuses which he had made to his uncle were certainly not valid. Some pretence at positively necessary routine duties it must be supposed that he made; but he spent more of his time either on the sea, or among the cliffs with Kate, or on the road going backwards and forwards, than he did at his quarters. It was known that he was to leave the regiment and become a great man at home in October, and his brother officers were kind to him. And it was known also, of course, that there was a young lady down on the sea coast beyond Ennistimon, and doubtless there were jokes on the subject. But there was no one with him at Ennis having such weight of fears or authority as might have served to help to rescue him. During this time Lady Mary Quin still made her reports, and his aunt's letters were full of cautions and entreaties. "I am told," said the Countess, in one of her now detested epistles, "that the young woman has a reprobate father who has escaped from the galleys. Oh, Fred, do not break our hearts." He had almost forgotten the Captain when he received this further rumour which had circulated to him round by Castle Quin and Scroope Manor.

It was all going from bad to worse. He was allowed by the mother to be at the cottage as much as he pleased, and the girl was allowed to wander with him when she would among the cliffs. It was so, although Father Marty himself had more than once cautioned Mrs. O'Hara that she was imprudent. "What can I do?" she said. "Have not you yourself taught me to believe that he is true?"

"Just spake a word to Miss Kate herself."

"What can I say to her now? She regards him as her husband before God."

"But he is not her husband in any way that would prevent his taking another wife an' he plases. And, believe me, Misthress O'Hara, them sort of young men like a girl a dale better when there's a little 'Stand off' about her."

"It is too late to bid her to be indifferent to him now, Father Marty."

161

"I am not saying that Miss Kate is to lose her lover. I hope I'll have the binding of 'em together myself, and I'll go bail I'll do it fast enough. In the meanwhile let her keep herself to herself a little more."

The advice was very good, but Mrs. O'Hara knew not how to make use of it. She could tell the young man that she would have his heart's blood if he deceived them, and she could look at him as though she meant to be as good as her word. She had courage enough for any great emergency. But now that the lover had been made free of the cottage she knew not how to debar him. She could not break her Kate's heart by expressing doubts to her. And were he to be told to stay away, would he not be lost to them for ever? Of course he could desert them if he would, and then they must die.

It was going from bad to worse certainly; and not the less so because he was more than ever infatuated about the girl. When he had calculated whether it might be possible to desert her he had been at Scroope. He was in County Clare now, and he did not hesitate to tell himself that it was impossible. Whatever might happen, and to whomever he might be false, — he would be true to her. He would at any rate be so true to her that he would not leave her. If he never made her his legal wife, his wife legal at all points, he would always treat her as wife. When his uncle the Earl should die, when the time came in which he would be absolutely free as to his own motions, he would discover the way in which this might best be done. If it were true that his Kate's father was a convict escaped from the galleys, that surely would be an additional reason why she should not be made Countess of Scroope. Even Mrs. O'Hara herself must understand that. With Kate, with his own Kate, he thought that there would be no difficulty.

From bad to worse! Alas, alas; there came a day in which the pricelessness of the girl he loved sank to nothing, vanished away, and was as a thing utterly lost, even in his eyes. The poor unfortunate one, — to whom beauty had been given, and grace, and softness, — and beyond all these and finer than these, innocence as unsullied as the whiteness of the plumage on the breast of a dove; but to whom, alas, had not been given a protector strong enough to protect her softness, or guardian wise enough to guard her innocence! To her he was godlike, noble, excellent, all but holy. He was the man whom Fortune, more than kind, had sent to her to be the joy of her existence, the fountain of her life, the strong staff for her weakness. Not to believe in him would be the foulest treason! To lose him would be to die! To deny him would be to deny her God! She gave him all; — and her pricelessness in his eyes was gone for ever.

He was sitting with her one day towards the end of May on the edge of the cliff, looking down upon the ocean and listening to the waves, when it occurred to him that he might as well ask her about her father. It was absurd he thought to stand upon any ceremony with her. He was very good to her, and intended to be always good to her, but it was essentially necessary to him to know the truth. He was not aware, perhaps, that he was becoming rougher with her than had been his wont. She certainly was not aware of it, though there was a touch of awe sometimes about her as she answered him. She was aware that she now shewed to him an absolute obedience in all things which had not been customary with her; but then it was so sweet to obey him; so happy a thing to have such a master! If he rebuked her, he did it with his arm round her waist, so that she could look into his face and smile as she promised that she would be good and follow his behests in all things. He had been telling her now of some fault in her dress, and she had been explaining that such faults would come when money was so scarce. Then he had offered her gifts. A gift she would of course take. She had already taken gifts which were the treasures of her heart. But he must not pay things for her till, — till —. Then she again looked up into his face and smiled. "You are not angry with me?" she said.

"Kate, — I want to ask you a particular question."

"What question?"

"You must not suppose, let the answer be what it may, that it can make any difference between you and me."

"Oh, — I hope not," she replied trembling.

"It shall make none," he answered with all a master's assurance and authority. "Therefore you need not be afraid to answer me. Tidings have reached me on a matter as to which I ought to be informed."

"What matter? Oh Fred, you do so frighten me. I'll tell you anything I know."

"I have been told that — that your father — is alive." He looked down upon her and could see that her face was red up to her very hair. "Your mother once told me that she had never been certain of his death."

"I used to think he was dead."

"But now you think he is alive?"

"I think he is; — but I do not know. I never saw my father so as to remember him; though I do remember that we used to be very unhappy when we were in Spain."

"And what have you heard lately? Tell me the truth, you know."

"Of course I shall tell you the truth, Fred. I think mother got a letter, but she did not shew it me. She said just a word, but nothing more. Father Marty will certainly know if she knows."

"And you know nothing?"

"Nothing."

"I think I must ask Father Marty."

"But will it matter to you?" Kate asked.

"At any rate it shall not matter to you," he said, kissing her. And then again she was happy; though there had now crept across her heart the shadow of some sad foreboding, a foretaste of sorrow that was not altogether bitter as sorrow is, but which taught her to cling closely to him when he was there and would fill her eyes with tears when she thought of him in his absence.

On this day he had not found Mrs. O'Hara at the cottage. She had gone down to Liscannor, Kate told him. He had sent his boat back to the strand near that village, round the point and into the bay, as it could not well lie under the rocks at high tide, and he now asked Kate to accompany him as he walked down. They would probably meet her mother on the road. Kate, as she tied on her hat, was only too happy to be his companion. "I think," he said, "that I shall try and see Father Marty as I go back. If your mother has really heard anything about your father, she ought to have told me."

"Don't be angry with mother, Fred."

"I won't be angry with you, my darling," said the master with masterful tenderness.

Although he had intimated his intention of calling on the priest that very afternoon, it may be doubted whether he was altogether gratified when he met the very man with Mrs. O'Hara close to the old burying ground. "Ah, Mr. Neville," said the priest, "and how's it all wid you this many a day?"

"The top of the morning to you thin, Father Marty," said Fred, trying to assume an Irish brogue. Nothing could be more friendly than the greeting. The old priest took off his hat to

Kate, and made a low bow, as though he should say, — to the future Countess of Scroope I owe a very especial respect. Mrs. O'Hara held her future son-in-law's hand for a moment, as though she might preserve him for her daughter by some show of affection on her own part. "And now, Misthress O'Hara," said the priest, "as I've got a companion to go back wid me, I'm thinking I'll not go up the hill any further." Then they parted, and Kate looked as though she were being robbed of her due because her lover could not give her one farewell kiss in the priest's presence.

CHAPTER II.
IS SHE TO BE YOUR WIFE?

"It's quite a sthranger you are, these days," said the priest, as soon as they had turned their backs upon the ladies.

"Well; yes. We haven't managed to meet since I came back; — have we?"

"I've been pretty constant at home, too. But you like them cliffs up there, better than the village no doubt."

"Metal more attractive, Father Marty," said Fred laughing; — "not meaning however any slight upon Liscannor or the Cork whisky."

"The Cork whisky is always to the fore, Mr. Neville. And how did you lave matters with your noble uncle?"

Neville at the present moment was anxious rather to speak of Kate's ignoble father than of his own noble uncle. He had declared his intention of making inquiry of Father Marty, and he thought that he should do so with something of a high hand. He still had that scheme in his head, and he might perhaps be better prepared to discuss it with the priest if he could first make this friend of the O'Hara family understand how much he, Neville, was personally injured by this "turning up" of a disreputable father. But, should he allow the priest at once to run away to Scroope and his noble uncle, the result of such conversation would simply be renewed promises on his part in reference to his future conduct to Kate O'Hara.

"Lord Scroope wasn't very well when I left him. By the bye, Father Marty, I've been particularly anxious to see you."

" 'Deed thin I was aisy found, Mr. Neville."

"What is this I hear about — Captain O'Hara?"

"What is it that you have heard, Mr. Neville?" Fred looked into the priest's face and found that he, at least, did not blush. It may be that all power of blushing had departed from Father Marty.

"In the first place I hear that there is such a man."

"Ony way there was once."

"You think he's dead then?"

"I don't say that. It's a matter of, — faith, thin, it's a matter of nigh twenty years since I saw the Captain. And when I did see him I didn't like him. I can tell you that, Mr. Neville."

"I suppose not."

"That lass up there was not born when I saw him. He was a handsome man too, and might have been a gentleman av' he would."

"But he wasn't."

"It's a hard thing to say what is a gentleman,

169

Mr. Neville. I don't know a much harder thing. Them folk at Castle Quin, now, wouldn't scruple to say that I'm no gentleman, just because I'm a Popish priest. I say that Captain O'Hara was no gentleman because — he ill-treated a woman." Father Marty as he said this stopped a moment on the road, turning round and looking Neville full in the face. Fred bore the look fairly well. Perhaps at the moment he did not understand its application. It may be that he still had a clear conscience in that matter, and thought that he was resolved to treat Kate O'Hara after a fashion that would in no way detract from his own character as a gentleman. "As it was," continued the priest, "he was a low blag-guard."

"He hadn't any money, I suppose?"

" 'Deed and I don't think he was iver throubled much in respect of money. But money doesn't matter, Mr. Neville."

"Not in the least," said Fred.

"Thim ladies up there are as poor as Job, but anybody that should say that they weren't ladies would just be shewing that he didn't know the difference. The Captain was well born, Mr. Neville, av' that makes ony odds."

"Birth does go for something, Father Marty."

"Thin let the Captain have the advantage. Them O'Haras of Kildare weren't proud of him I'm thinking, but he was a chip of that block; and some one belonging to him had seen the errors of the family ways, in respect of making him a Papist. 'Deed and I must say, Mr. Neville,

when they send us any offsets from a Prothes-
tant family it isn't the best that they give us."

"I suppose not, Father Marty."

"We can make something of a bit of wood that
won't take ony shape at all, at all along wid
them. But there wasn't much to boast of along
of the Captain."

"But is he alive, Father Marty; — or is he
dead? I think I've a right to be told."

"I am glad to hear you ask it as a right, Mr.
Neville. You have a right if that young lady up
there is to be your wife." Fred made no answer
here, though the priest paused for a moment,
hoping that he would do so. But the question
could be asked again, and Father Marty went on
to tell all that he knew, and all that he had heard
of Captain O'Hara. He was alive. Mrs. O'Hara
had received a letter purporting to be from her
husband, giving an address in London, and asking for money. He, Father Marty, had seen the
letter; and he thought that there might perhaps
be a doubt whether it was written by the man of
whom they were speaking. Mrs. O'Hara had
declared that if it were so written the handwriting was much altered. But then in twelve years
the writing of a man who drank hard will
change. It was twelve years since she had last
received a letter from him.

"And what do you believe?"

"I think he lives, and that he wrote it, Mr.
Neville. I'll tell you God's truth about it as I
believe it, because as I said before, I think you

are entitled to know the truth."

"And what was done?"

"I sent off to London, — to a friend I have."

"And what did your friend say?"

"He says there is a man calling himself Captain O'Hara."

"And is that all?"

"She got a second letter. She got it the very last day you was down here. Pat Cleary took it up to her when you was out wid Miss Kate."

"He wants money, I suppose."

"Just that, Mr. Neville."

"It makes a difference; — doesn't it?"

"How does it make a difference?"

"Well; it does. I wonder you don't see it. You must see it." From that moment Father Marty said in his heart that Kate O'Hara had lost her husband. Not that he admitted for a moment that Captain O'Hara's return, if he had returned, would justify the lover in deserting the girl; but that he perceived that Neville had already allowed himself to entertain the plea. The whole affair had in the priest's estimation been full of peril; but then the prize to be won was very great! From the first he had liked the young man, and had not doubted, — did not now doubt, — but that if once married he would do justice to his wife. Even though Kate should fail and should come out of the contest with a scorched heart, — and that he had thought more than probable, — still the prize was very high and the girl he thought was one who could survive such a blow. Latterly, in that respect he had changed his opinion. Kate had shewn herself to be capable of so deep a passion that he was now sure that she would be more than scorched should the fire be one to injure and not to cherish her. But the man's promises had been so firm, so often reiterated, were so clearly written, that the priest had almost dared to hope that the thing was assured. Now, alas, he perceived that the embryo English lord was already looking for a means of escape, and already thought that he had found it in this unfortunate return of the father. The whole extent of the sorrow even the priest did not know. But he was determined to fight the battle to the very last. The man should make the girl his wife, or he, Father Marty, parish priest of Liscannor, would know the reason why. He was a man who was wont to desire to know the reason why, as to matters which he had taken in hand. But when he heard the words which Neville spoke and marked the tone in which they were uttered he felt that the young man was preparing for himself a way of escape.

"I don't see that it should make any difference," he said shortly.

"If the man be disreputable, —"

"The daughter is not therefore disreputable. Her position is not changed."

"I have to think of my friends."

"You should have thought of that before you declared yourself to her, Mr. Neville." How true this was now, the young man knew better than the priest, but that, as yet, was his own secret. "You do not mean to tell me that because the father is not all that he should be, she is therefore to be thrown over. That cannot be your idea of honour. Have you not promised that you would make her your wife?" The priest stopped for an answer, but the young man made him none. "Of course you have promised her."

"I suppose she has told you so."

"To whom should she tell her story? To whom should she go for advice? But it was you who told me so, yourself."

"Never."

"Did you not swear to me that you would not injure her? And why should there have been any talk with you and me about her, but that I saw what was coming? When a young man like you chooses to spend his hours day after day and week after week with such a one as she is, with a beautiful young girl, a sweet innocent young lady, so sweet as to make even an ould priest like me feel that the very atmosphere she breathes is perfumed and hallowed, must it not mean one of two things; — that he desires to make her his wife or else, — or else something so vile that I will not name it in connection with Kate O'Hara? Then as her mother's friend, and as hers, — as their only friend near them, I spoke out plainly to you, and you swore to me that you intended no harm to her."

"I would not harm her for the world."

"When you said that, you told me as plainly as you could spake that she should be your wife. With her own mouth she never told me. Her mother has told me. Daily Mrs. O'Hara has spoken to me of her hopes and fears. By the Lord above me whom I worship, and by His Son in whom I rest all my hopes, I would not stand in your shoes if you intend to tell that woman that after all that has passed you mean to desert her child."

"Who has talked of deserting?" asked Neville angrily.

"Say that you will be true to her, that you will make her your wife before God and man, and I will humbly ask your pardon."

"All that I say is that this Captain O'Hara's coming is a nuisance."

"If that be all, there is an end of it. It is a nuisance. Not that I suppose he ever will come. If he persists she must send him a little money. There shall be no difficulty about that. She will never ask you to supply the means of keeping her husband."

"It isn't the money. I think you hardly understand my position, Father Marty." It seemed to Neville that if it was ever his intention to open out his scheme to the priest, now was his time for doing so. They had come to the cross roads at which one way led down to the village and to Father Marty's house, and the other to the spot on the beach where the boat would be waiting.

175

"I can't very well go on to Liscannor," said Neville.

"Give me your word before we part that you will keep your promise to Miss O'Hara," said the priest.

"If you will step on a few yards with me I will tell you just how I am situated." Then the priest assented, and they both went on towards the beach, walking very slowly. "If I alone were concerned, I would give up everything for Miss O'Hara. I am willing to give up everything as regards myself. I love her so dearly that she is more to me than all the honours and wealth that are to come to me when my uncle dies."

"What is to hinder but that you should have the girl you love and your uncle's honours and wealth into the bargain?"

"That is just it."

"By the life of me I don't see any difficulty. You're your own masther. The ould Earl can't disinherit you if he would."

"But I am bound down."

"How bound? Who can bind you?"

"I am bound not to make Miss O'Hara Countess of Scroope."

"What binds you? You are bound by a hundred promises to make her your wife."

"I have taken an oath that no Roman Catholic shall become Countess Scroope as my wife."

"Then, Mr. Neville, let me tell you that you must break your oath."

"Would you have me perjure myself?"

"Faith I would. Perjure yourself one way you certainly must, av' you've taken such an oath as that, for you've sworn many oaths that you would make this Catholic lady your wife. Not make a Roman Catholic Countess of Scroope! It's the impudence of some of you Prothestants that kills me entirely. As though we couldn't count Countesses against you and beat you by chalks! I ain't the man to call hard names, Mr. Neville; but if one of us is upstarts, it's aisy seeing which. Your uncle's an ould man, and I'm told nigh to his latter end. I'm not saying but what you should respect even his wakeness. But you'll not look me in the face and tell me that afther what's come and gone that young lady is to be cast on one side like a plucked rose, because an ould man has spoken a foolish word, or because a young man has made a wicked promise."

They were now standing again, and Fred raised his hat and rubbed his forehead as he endeavoured to arrange the words in which he could best propose his scheme to the priest. He had not yet escaped from the idea that because Father Marty was a Roman Catholic priest, living in a village in the extreme west of Ireland, listening night and day to the roll of the Atlantic and drinking whisky punch, therefore he would be found to be romantic, semi-barbarous, and perhaps more than semi-lawless in his views of life. Irish priests have been made by chroniclers of Irish story to do marvellous things; and Fred

177

Neville thought that this priest, if only the matter could be properly introduced, might be persuaded to do for him something romantic, something marvellous, perhaps something almost lawless. In truth it might have been difficult to find a man more practical or more honest than Mr. Marty. And then the difficulty of introducing the subject was very great. Neville stood with his face a little averted, rubbing his forehead as he raised his sailor's hat. "If you could only read my heart," he said, "you'd know that I am as true as steel."

"I'd be lothe to doubt it, Mr. Neville."

"I'd give up everything to call Kate my own."

"But you need give up nothing, and yet have her all your own."

"You say that because you don't completely understand. It may as well be taken for granted at once that she can never be Countess of Scroope."

"Taken for granted!" said the old man as the fire flashed out of his eyes.

"Just listen to me for one moment. I will marry her to-morrow, or at any time you may fix, if a marriage can be so arranged that she shall never be more than Mrs. Neville."

"And what would you be?"

"Mr. Neville."

"And what would her son be?"

"Oh; — just the same, — when he grew up. Perhaps there wouldn't be a son."

"God forbid that there should on those terms.

You intend that your children and her children shall be — bastards. That's about it, Mr. Neville." The romance seemed to vanish when the matter was submitted to him in this very prosaic manner. "As to what you might choose to call yourself, that would be nothing to me and not very much I should say, to her. I believe a man needn't be a lord unless he likes to be a lord; — and needn't call his wife a countess. But, Mr. Neville, when you have married Miss O'Hara, and when your uncle shall have died, there can be no other Countess of Scroope, and her child must be the heir to your uncle's title."

"All that I could give her except that, she should have."

"But she must have that. She must be your wife before God and man, and her children must be the children of honour and not of disgrace." Ah, — if the priest had known it all!

"I would live abroad with her, and her mother should live with us."

"You mean that you would take Kate O'Hara as your misthress! And you make this as a proposal to me! Upon my word, Mr. Neville, I don't think that I quite understand what it is that you're maning to say to me. Is she to be your wife?"

"Yes," said Neville, urged by the perturbation of his spirit to give a stronger assurance than he had intended.

"Then must her son if she have one be the future Earl of Scroope. He may be Protesthant,

179

— or what you will?"

"You don't understand me, Father Marty."

"Faith, and that's thrue. But we are at the baich, Mr. Neville, and I've two miles along the coast to Liscannor."

"Shall I make Barney take you round in the canoe?"

"I believe I may as well walk it. Good-bye, Mr. Neville. I'm glad at any rate to hear you say so distinctly that you are resolved at all hazards to make that dear girl your wife." This he said, almost in a whisper, standing close to the boat, with his hand on Neville's shoulder. He paused a moment as though to give special strength to his words, and Neville did not dare or was not able to protest against the assertion. Father Marty himself was certainly not romantic in his manner of managing such an affair as this in which they were now both concerned.

Neville went back to Ennis much depressed, turning the matter over in his mind almost hopelessly. This was what had come from his adventures! No doubt he might marry the girl, — postponing his marriage till after his uncle's death. For aught he knew as yet that might still be possible. But were he to do so, he would disgrace his family, and disgrace himself by breaking the solemn promise he had made. And in such case he would be encumbered, and possibly be put beyond the pale of that sort of life which should be his as Earl of Scroope, by having Captain O'Hara as his father-in-law. He was

180

aware now that he would be held by all his natural friends to have ruined himself by such a marriage.

On the other hand he could, no doubt, throw the girl over. They could not make him marry her though they could probably make him pay very dearly for not doing so. If he could only harden his heart sufficiently he could escape in that way. But he was not hard, and he did feel that so escaping, he would have a load on his breast which would make his life unendurable. Already he was beginning to hate the coast of Ireland, and to think that the gloom of Scroope Manor was preferable to it.

CHAPTER III.
FRED NEVILLE
RECEIVES A VISITOR
AT ENNIS.

For something over three weeks after his walk
with the priest Neville saw neither of the two
ladies of Ardkill. Letters were frequent between
the cottage and the barracks at Ennis, but, — so
said Fred himself, military duties detained him
with the troop. He explained that he had been
absent a great deal, and that now Captain
Johnstone was taking his share of ease. He was
all alone at the barracks, and could not get away.
There was some truth in this, created perhaps
by the fact that as he didn't stir, Johnstone could
do so. Johnstone was backwards and forwards,
fishing at Castle Connel, and Neville was very
exact in explaining that for the present he was
obliged to give up all the delights of the coast.
But the days were days of trial to him.

A short history of the life of Captain O'Hara
was absolutely sent to him by the Countess of
Scroope. The family lawyer, at the instance of
the Earl, — as she said, though probably her
own interference had been more energetic than
that of the Earl, — had caused enquiries to be
made. Captain O'Hara, the husband of the lady

who was now living on the coast of County Clare, and who was undoubtedly the father of the Miss O'Hara whom Fred knew, had passed at least ten of the latter years of his life at the galleys in the south of France. He had been engaged in an extensive swindling transaction at Bordeaux, and had thence been transferred to Toulon, had there been maintained by France, — and was now in London. The Countess in sending this interesting story to her nephew at Ennis, with ample documentary evidence, said that she was sure that he would not degrade his family utterly by thinking of allying himself with people who were so thoroughly disreputable; but that, after all that was passed, his uncle expected from him a renewed assurance on the matter. He answered this in anger. He did not understand why the history of Captain O'Hara should have been raked up. Captain O'Hara was nothing to him. He supposed it had come from Castle Quin, and anything from Castle Quin he disbelieved. He had given a promise once and he didn't understand why he should be asked for any further assurance. He thought it very hard that his life should be made a burden to him by foul-mouthed rumours from Castle Quin. That was the tenour of his letter to his aunt; but even that letter sufficed to make it almost certain that he could never marry the girl. He acknowledged that he had bound himself not to do so. And then, in spite of all that he said about the mendacity of Castle Quin, he did believe the little history. And it was quite out of the question that he should marry the daughter of a returned galley-slave. He did not think that any jury in England would hold him to be bound by such a promise. Of course he would do whatever he could for his dear Kate; but, even after all that had passed, he could not pollute himself by marriage with the child of so vile a father. Poor Kate! Her sufferings would have been occasioned not by him, but by her father.

In the meantime Kate's letters to him became more and more frequent, more and more sad, — filled ever with still increasing warmth of entreaty. At last they came by every post, though he knew how difficult it must be for her to find daily messengers into Ennistimon. Would he not come and see her? He must come and see her. She was ill and would die unless he came to her. He did not always answer these letters, but he did write to her perhaps twice a week. He would come very soon, — as soon as Johnstone had come back from his fishing. She was not to fret herself. Of course he could not always be at Ardkill. He too had things to trouble him. Then he told her he had received letters from home which caused him very much trouble; and there was a something of sharpness in his words, which brought from her a string of lamentations in which, however, the tears and wailings did not as yet take the form of reproaches. Then there came a short note from Mrs. O'Hara herself. "I must beg that you will come to Ardkill at once. It is absolutely necessary for Kate's safety that you should do so."

When he received this he thought that he would go on the morrow. When the morrow came he determined to postpone the journey another day! The calls of duty are so much less imperious than those of pleasure! On that further day he still meant to go, as he sat about noon unbraced, only partly dressed in his room at the barracks. His friend Johnstone was back in Ennis, and there was also a Cornet with the troop. He had no excuse whatever on the score of military duty for remaining at home on that day. But he sat idling his time, thinking of things. All the charm of the adventure was gone. He was sick of the canoe and of Barney Morony. He did not care a straw for the seals or wild gulls. The moaning of the ocean beneath the cliff was no longer pleasurable to him, — and as to the moaning at their summit, to tell the truth, he was afraid of it. The long drive thither and back was tedious to him. He thought now more of the respectability of his family than of the beauty of Kate O'Hara.

But still he meant to go, — certainly would go on this very day. He had desired that his gig should be ready, and had sent word to say that he might start at any moment. But still he sat in his dressing-gown at noon, unbraced, with a novel in his hand which he could not read, and a pipe by his side which he could not smoke.

Close to him on the table lay that record of the life of Captain O'Hara, which his aunt had sent him, every word of which he had now examined for the third or fourth time. Of course he could not marry the girl. Mrs. O'Hara had deceived him. She could not but have known that her husband was a convict; — and had kept the knowledge back from him in order that she might allure him to the marriage. Anything that money could do, he would do. Or, if they would consent, he would take the girl away with him to some sunny distant clime, in which adventures might still be sweet, and would then devote to her — some portion of his time. He had not yet ruined himself, but he would indeed ruin himself were he, the heir to the earldom of Scroope, to marry the daughter of a man who had been at the French galleys! He had just made up his mind that he would be firm in this resolution, — when the door opened and Mrs. O'Hara entered his room. "Mrs. O'Hara."

She closed the door carefully behind her before she spoke, excluding the military servant who had wished to bar her entrance. "Yes, sir; as you would not come to us I have been forced to come to you. I know it all. When will you make my child your wife?"

Yes. In the abjectness of her misery the poor girl had told her mother the story of her disgrace; or, rather, in her weakness had suffered her secret to fall from her lips. That terrible retribution was to come upon her which, when sin has been mutual, falls with so crushing a weight upon her who of the two sinners has ever been by far the less sinful. She, when she knew her doom, simply found herself bound by still stronger ties of love to him who had so cruelly injured her. She was his before; but now she was more than ever his. To have him near her, to give her orders that she might obey them, was the consolation that she coveted, — the only consolation that could have availed anything to her. To lean against him, and to whisper to him, with face averted, with half-formed syllables, some fervent words that might convey to him a truth which might be almost a joy to her if he would make it so, — was the one thing that could restore hope to her bosom. Let him come and be near to her, so that she might hide her face upon his breast. But he came not. He did not come, though, as best she knew how, she had thrown all her heart into her letters. Then her spirit sank within her, and she sickened, and as her mother knelt over her, she allowed her secret to fall from her.

Fred Neville's sitting-room at Ennis was not a chamber prepared for the reception of ladies. It was very rough, as are usually barrack rooms in outlying quarters in small towns in the west of Ireland, — and it was also very untidy. The more prudent and orderly of mankind might hardly have understood why a young man, with prospects and present wealth such as belonged to Neville, should choose to spend a twelvemonth in such a room, contrary to the wishes of all his friends, when London was open to him, and the continent, and scores of the best appointed houses in England, and all the glories of owner-ship at Scroope. There were guns about, and whips, hardly half a dozen books, and a few papers. There were a couple of swords lying on a table that looked like a dresser. The room was not above half covered with its carpet, and though there were three large easy chairs, even they were torn and soiled. But all this had been compatible with adventures, — and while the adventures were simply romantic and not a bit troublesome, the barracks at Ennis had been to him by far preferable to the gloomy grandeur of Scroope.

And now Mrs. O'Hara was there, telling him that she knew of all! Not for a moment did he remain ignorant of the meaning of her com-munication. And now the arguments to be used against him in reference to the marriage would be stronger than ever. A silly, painful smile came across his handsome face as he attempted to welcome her, and moved a chair for her accom-modation. "I am so sorry that you have had the trouble of coming over," he said.

"That is nothing. When will you make my child your wife?" How was he to answer this? In the midst of his difficulties he had brought himself to one determination. He had resolved that under no pressure would he marry the daughter of O'Hara, the galley-slave. As far as that, he had seen his way. Should he now at once speak of the galley-slave, and, with expressions of regret, decline the alliance on that reason? Having dishonoured this woman's daughter should he shelter himself behind the dishonour of her husband? That he meant to do so ultimately is true; but at the present moment such a task would have required a harder heart than his. She rose from her chair and stood close over him as she repeated her demand, "When will you make my child your wife?"

"You do not want me to answer you at this moment?"

"Yes; — at this moment. Why not answer me at once? She has told me all. Mr. Neville, you must think not only of her, but of your child also."

"I hope not that," he said.

"I tell you that it is so. Now answer me. When shall my Kate become your wife?"

He still knew that any such consummation as that was quite out of the question. The mother herself as she was now present to him, seemed to be a woman very different from the quiet, handsome, high-spirited, but low-voiced widow whom he had known, or thought that he had known, at Ardkill. Of her as she had there appeared to him he had not been ashamed to think as one who might at some future time be personally related to himself. He had recognized her as a lady whose outward trappings, poor though they might be, were suited to the seclusion in which she lived. But now, although it was only to Ennis that she had come from her nest among the rocks, she seemed to be unfitted for even so much intercourse with the world as that. And in the demand which she reiterated over him she hardly spoke as a lady would speak. Would not all they who were connected with him at home have a right to complain if he were to bring such a woman with him to England as the mother of his wife. "I can't answer such a question as that on the spur of the moment," he said.

"You will not dare to tell me that you mean to desert her?"

"Certainly not. I was coming over to Ardkill this very day. The trap is ordered. I hope Kate is well?"

"She is not well. How should she be well?"

"Why not? I didn't know. If there is anything that she wants that I can get for her, you have only to speak."

In the utter contempt which Mrs. O'Hara now felt for the man she probably forgot that his immediate situation was one in which it was nearly impossible that any man should conduct himself with dignity. Having brought himself to his present pass by misconduct, he could discover no line of good conduct now open to him. Moralists might tell him that let the girl's parentage be what it might, he ought to marry her; but he was stopped from that, not only by his oath, but by a conviction that his highest duty required him to preserve his family from degradation.

And yet to a mother, with such a demand on her lips as that now made by Mrs. O'Hara, — whose demand was backed by such circumstances, — how was it possible that he should tell the truth and plead the honour of his family? His condition was so cruel that it was no longer possible to him to be dignified or even true. The mother again made her demand. "There is one thing that you must do for her before other things can be thought of. When shall she become your wife?"

It was for a moment on his tongue to tell her that it could not be so while his uncle lived; — but to this he at once felt that there were two objections, directly opposed to each other, but each so strong as to make any such reply very dangerous. It would imply a promise, which he certainly did not intend to keep, of marrying the girl when his uncle should be dead; and, although promising so much more than he intended to perform, would raise the ungovernable wrath of the woman before him. That he should now hesitate, — now, in her Kate's present condition, — as to redeeming those vows of marriage which he had made to her in her innocence, would raise a fury in the mother's bosom which he feared to encounter. He got up and walked about the room, while she stood with her eyes fixed upon him, ever and anon reiterating her demand. "No day must now be lost. When will you make my child your wife?"

At last he made a proposition to which she assented. The tidings which she had brought him had come upon him very suddenly. He was inexpressibly pained. Of course Kate, his dearest Kate, was everything to him. Let him have that afternoon to think about it. On the morrow he would assuredly visit Ardkill. The mother, full of fears, resolving that should he attempt to play her girl false and escape from her she would follow him to the end of the world, but feeling that at the present moment she could not constrain him, accepted his repeated promise as to the following day; and at last left him to himself.

Chapter IV.
Neville's Success.

Neville sat in his room alone, without moving, for a couple of hours after Mrs. O'Hara had left him. In what way should he escape from the misery and ruin which seemed to surround him? An idea did cross his mind that it would be better for him to fly and write the truth from the comparatively safe distance of his London club. But there would be a meanness in such conduct which would make it impossible that he should ever again hold up his head. The girl had trusted to him, and by trusting to him had brought herself to this miserable pass. He could not desert her. It would be better that he should go and endure all the vials of their wrath than that. To her he would still be tenderly loving, if she would accept his love without the name which he could not give her. His whole life he would sacrifice to her. Every luxury which money could purchase he would lavish on her. He must go and make his offer. The vials of wrath which would doubtless be poured out upon his head would not come from her. In his heart of hearts he feared both the priest and the mother. But

193

there are moments in which a man feels himself obliged to encounter all that he most fears; — and the man who does not do so in such moments is a coward.

He quite made up his mind to start early on the following morning; but the intermediate hours were very sad and heavy, and his whole outlook into life was troublesome to him. How infinitely better would it have been for him had he allowed himself to be taught a twelvemonth since that his duty required him to give up the army at once! But he had made his bed, and now he must lie upon it. There was no escape from this journey to Ardkill. Even though he should be stunned by their wrath he must endure it.

He breakfasted early the next day, and got into his gig before nine. He must face the enemy, and the earlier that he did it the better. His difficulty now lay in arranging the proposition that he would make and the words that he should speak. Every difficulty would be smoothed and every danger dispelled if he would only say that he would marry the girl as quickly as the legal forms would allow. Father Marty, he knew, would see to all that, and the marriage might be done effectually. He had quite come to understand that Father Marty was practical rather than romantic. But there would be cowardice in this as mean as that other cowardice. He believed himself to be bound by his duty to his family. Were he now to renew his promise of marriage, such renewal would be caused by fear and not by duty, and would be mean. They should tear him piecemeal rather than get from him such a promise. Then he thought of the Captain, and perceived that he must make all possible use of the Captain's character. Would anybody conceive that he, the heir of the Scroope family, was bound to marry the daughter of a convict returned from the galleys? And was it not true that such promise as he had made had been obtained under false pretences? Why had he not been told of the Captain's position when he first made himself intimate with the mother and daughter?

Instead of going as was his custom to Lahinch, and then rowing across the bay and round the point, he drove his gig to the village of Liscannor. He was sick of Barney Morony and the canoe, and never desired to see either of them again. He was sick indeed, of everything Irish, and thought that the whole island was a mistake. He drove however boldly through Liscannor and up to Father Marty's yard, and, not finding the priest at home, there left his horse and gig. He had determined that he would first go to the priest and boldly declare that nothing should induce him to marry the daughter of a convict. But Father Marty was not at home. The old woman who kept his house believed that he had gone into Ennistown. He was away with his horse, and would not be back till dinner time. Then Neville, having seen his own nag taken from the gig, started on his walk up to Ardkill.

How ugly the country was to his eyes as he now saw it. Here and there stood a mud cabin, and the small, half-cultivated fields, or rather patches of land, in which the thin oat crops were beginning to be green, were surrounded by low loose ramshackle walls, which were little more than heaps of stone, so carelessly had they been built and so negligently preserved. A few cocks and hens with here and there a miserable, starved pig seemed to be the stock of the country. Not a tree, not a shrub, not a flower was there to be seen. The road was narrow, rough, and unused. The burial ground which he passed was the liveliest sign of humanity about the place. Then the country became still wilder, and there was no road. The oats also ceased, and the walls. But he could hear the melancholy moan of the waves, which he had once thought to be musical and had often sworn that he loved. Now the place with all its attributes was hideous to him, distasteful, and abominable. At last the cottage was in view, and his heart sank very low. Poor Kate! He loved her dearly through it all. He endeavoured to take comfort by assuring himself that his heart was true to her. Not for worlds would he injure her; — that is, not for worlds, had any worlds been exclusively his own. On account of the Scroope world, — which was a world general rather than particular, — no doubt he must injure her most horribly. But still she was his dear Kate, his own Kate, his Kate whom he would never desert.

When he came up to the cottage the little gate was open, and he knew that somebody was there besides the usual inmates. His heart at once told him that it was the priest. His fate had brought him face to face with his two enemies at once! His breath almost left him, but he knew that he could not run away. However bitter might be the vials of wrath he must encounter them. So he knocked at the outer door and, after his custom, walked into the passage. Then he knocked again at the door of the one sitting-room, — the door which hitherto he had always passed with the conviction that he should bring delight, — and for a moment there was no answer. He heard no voice and he knocked again. The door was opened for him, and as he entered he met Father Marty. But he at once saw that there was another man in the room, seated in an arm chair near the window. Kate, his Kate, was not there, but Mrs. O'Hara was standing at the head of the sofa, far away from the window and close to the door. "It is Mr. Neville," said the priest. "It is as well that he should come in."

"Mr. Neville," said the man rising from his chair, "I am informed that you are a suitor for the hand of my daughter. Your prospects in life are sufficient, sir, and I give my consent."

The man was a thing horrible to look at, tall, thin, cadaverous, ill-clothed, with his wretched and all but ragged overcoat buttoned close up to his chin, with long straggling thin grizzled hair, red-nosed, with a drunkard's eyes, and thin lips drawn down at the corners of the mouth. This was Captain O'Hara; and if any man ever looked like a convict returned from work in chains, such was the appearance of this man. This was the father of Fred's Kate; — the man whom it was expected that he, Frederic Neville, the future Earl of Scroope, should take as his father-in-law! "This is Captain O'Hara," said the priest. But even Father Marty, bold as he was, could not assume the voice with which he had rebuked Neville as he walked with him, now nearly a month ago, down to the beach.

Neville did feel that the abomination of the man's appearance strengthened his position. He stood looking from one to another, while Mrs. O'Hara remained silent in the corner. "Perhaps," said he, "I had better not be here. I am intruding."

"It is right that you should know it all," said the priest. "As regards the young lady it cannot now alter your position. This gentleman must be — arranged for."

"Oh, certainly," said the Captain. "I must be — arranged for, and that so soon as possible." The man spoke with a slightly foreign accent and in a tone, as Fred thought, which savoured altogether of the galleys. "You have done me the honour, I am informed, to make my daughter all your own. These estimable people assure me that you hasten to make her your wife on the instant. I consent. The O'Haras, who are of the very oldest blood in Europe, have always connected themselves highly. Your uncle is a most excellent nobleman whose hand I shall be proud to grasp." As he thus spoke he stalked across the room to Fred, intending at once to commence the work of grasping the Neville family.

"Get back," said Fred, retreating to the door.

"Is it that you fail to believe that I am your bride's father?"

"I know not whose father you may be. Get back."

"He is what he says he is," said the priest. "You should bear with him for a while."

"Where is Kate?" demanded Fred. It seemed as though, for the moment, he were full of courage. He looked round at Mrs. O'Hara, but nobody answered him. She was still standing with her eyes fixed upon the man, almost as though she thought that she could dart out upon him and destroy him. "Where is Kate?" he asked again. "Is she well?"

"Well enough to hide herself from her old father," said the Captain, brushing a tear from his eye with the back of his hand.

"You shall see her presently, Mr. Neville," said the priest.

Then Neville whispered a word into the priest's ear. "What is it that the man wants?"

"You need not regard that," said Father Marty.

"Mr. Marty," said the Captain, "you concern yourself too closely in my affairs. I prefer to open my thoughts and desires to my son-in-law. He has taken measures which give him a right to interfere in the family. Ha, ha, ha."

"If you talk like that I'll stab you to the heart," said Mrs. O'Hara, jumping forward. Then Fred Neville perceived that the woman had a dagger in her hand which she had hitherto concealed from him as she stood up against the wall behind the head of the sofa. He learnt afterwards that the priest, having heard in Liscannor of the man's arrival, had hurried up to the cottage, reaching it almost at the same moment with the Captain. Kate had luckily at the moment been in her room and had not seen her father. She was still in her bed and was ill; — but during the scene that occurred afterwards she roused herself. But Mrs. O'Hara, even in the priest's presence, had at once seized the weapon from the drawer, — showing that she was prepared even for murder, had murder been found necessary by her for her relief. The man had immediately asked as to the condition of his daughter, and the mother had learned that her child's secret was known to all Liscannor. The priest now laid his hand upon her and stopped her, but he did it in all gentleness. "You'll have a fierce pig of a mother-in-law, Mr. Neville," said the Captain, "but your wife's father, — you'll find him always gentle and open to reason. You were asking what I wanted."

"Had I not better give him money?" suggested Neville.

"No," said the priest shaking his head.

"Certainly," said Captain O'Hara.

"If you will leave this place at once," said Neville, "and come to me to-morrow morning at the Ennis barracks, I will give you money."

"Give him none," said Mrs. O'Hara.

"My beloved is unreasonable. You would not be rid of me even were he to be so hard. I should not die. Have I not proved to you that I am one whom it is hard to destroy by privation. The family has been under a cloud. A day of sunshine has come with this gallant young nobleman. Let me partake the warmth. I will visit you, Mr. Neville, certainly; — but what shall be the figure?"

"That will be as I shall find you then."

"I will trust you. I will come. The journey hence to Ennis is long for one old as I am, and would be lightened by so small a trifle as — shall I say a bank note of the meanest value." Upon this Neville handed him two bank notes for £1 each, and Captain O'Hara walked forth out of his wife's house.

"He will never leave you now," said the priest.

"He cannot hurt me. I will arrange with some man of business to pay him a stipend as long as he never troubles our friend here. Though all the world should know it, will it not be better so?"

Great and terrible is the power of money. When this easy way out of their immediate difficulties had been made by the rich man, even Mrs. O'Hara with all her spirit was subdued for the moment, and the reproaches of the priest were silenced for that hour. The young man had seemed to behave well, had stood up as the friend of the suffering women, and had been at any rate ready with his money. "And now," he said, "where is Kate?" Then Mrs. O'Hara took him by the hand and led him into the bedroom in which the poor girl had buried herself from her father's embrace. "Is he gone?" she asked before even she would throw herself into her lover's arms.

"Neville has paid him money," said the mother.

"Yes, he has gone," said Fred; "and I think, — I think that he will trouble you no more."

"Oh, Fred, oh, my darling, oh, my own one. At last, at last you have come to me. Why have you stayed away? You will not stay away again? Oh, Fred, you do love me? Say that you love me."

"Better than all the world," he said pressing her to his bosom.

He remained with her for a couple of hours, during which hardly a word was said to him about his marriage. So great had been the effect upon them all of the sudden presence of the Captain, and so excellent had been the service rendered them by the trust which the Captain had placed in the young man's wealth, that for this day both priest and mother were incapacitated from making their claim with the vigour and intensity of purpose which they would have shewn had Captain O'Hara not presented himself at the cottage. The priest left them soon, — but not till it had been arranged that Neville should go back to Ennis to prepare for his reception of the Captain, and return to the cottage on the day after that interview was over. He assumed on a sudden the practical views of a man of business. He would take care to have an Ennis attorney with him when speaking to the Captain, and would be quite prepared to go to the extent of two hundred a year for the Captain's life, if the Captain could be safely purchased for that money. "A quarter of it would do," said Mrs. O'Hara. The priest thought £2 a week would be ample. "I'll be as good as my word," said Fred. Kate sat looking into his face thinking that he was still a god.

"And you will certainly be here by noon on Sunday?" said Kate, clinging to him when he rose to go.

"Most certainly."

"Dear, dear Fred." And so he walked down the hill to the priest's house almost triumphantly. He thought himself fortunate in not finding the priest who had ridden off from Ardkill to some distant part of the parish; — and then drove himself back to Ennis.

CHAPTER V.
FRED NEVILLE IS
AGAIN CALLED HOME
TO SCROOPE.

Neville was intent upon business, and had not been back in Ennis from the cottage half an hour before he obtained an introduction to an attorney. He procured it through the sergeant-major of the troop. The sergeant-major was intimate with the innkeeper, and the innkeeper was able to say that Mr. Thaddeus Crowe was an honest, intelligent, and peculiarly successful lawyer. Before he sat down to dinner Fred Neville was closeted at the barracks with Mr. Crowe.

He began by explaining to Mr. Crowe who he was. This he did in order that the attorney might know that he had the means of carrying out his purpose. Mr. Crowe bowed, and assured his client that on that score he had no doubts whatever. Nevertheless Mr. Crowe's first resolve, when he heard of the earldom and of the golden prospects, was to be very careful not to pay any money out of his own pocket on behalf of the young officer, till he made himself quite sure that it would be returned to him with interest. As the interview progressed, however, Mr.

Crowe began to see his way, and to understand that the golden prospects were not pleaded because the owner of them was himself short of cash. Mr. Crowe soon understood the whole story. He had heard of Captain O'Hara, and believed the man to be as thorough a blackguard as ever lived. When Neville told the attorney of the two ladies, and of the anxiety which he felt to screen them from the terrible annoyance of the Captain's visits, Mr. Crowe smiled, but made no remark. "It will be enough for you to know that I am in earnest about it," said the future Earl, resenting even the smile. Mr. Crowe bowed, and asked his client to finish the story. "The man is to be with me to-morrow, here, at twelve, and I wish you to be present. Mr. Crowe, my intention is to give him two hundred pounds a year as long as he lives."

"Two hundred a year!" said the Ennis attorney, to whom such an annuity seemed to be exorbitant as the purchase-money for a returned convict.

"Yes; — I have already mentioned that sum to his wife, though not to him."

"I should reconsider it, Mr. Neville."

"Thank you; — but I have made up my mind. The payments will be made of course only on condition that he troubles neither of the ladies either personally or by letter. It might be provided that it shall be paid to him weekly in France, but will not be paid should he leave that country. You will think of all this, and will make suggestions to-morrow. I shall be glad to have the whole thing left in your hands, so that I need simply remit the cheques to you. Perhaps I shall have the pleasure of seeing you to-morrow at twelve." Mr. Crowe promised to turn the matter over in his mind and to be present at the hour named. Neville carried himself very well through the interview, assuming with perfect ease the manners of the great and rich man who had only to give his orders with a certainty that they would be obeyed. Mr. Crowe, when he went out from the young man's presence, had no longer any doubt on his mind as to his client's pecuniary capability.

On the following day at twelve o'clock, Captain O'Hara, punctual to the minute, was at the barracks; and there also sitting in Neville's room, was the attorney. But Neville himself was not there, and the Captain immediately felt that he had been grossly imposed upon and swindled. "And who may I have the honour of addressing, when I speak to you, sir?" demanded the Captain.

"I am a lawyer."

"And Mr. Neville, — my own son-in-law, — has played me that trick!"

Mr. Crowe explained that no trick had been played, but did so in language which was no doubt less courteous than would have been used had Mr. Neville been present. As, however, the cause of our hero's absence is more important to us than the Captain's prospects that must be first explained.

As soon as the attorney left him Neville had sat down to dinner with his two brother officers, but was not by any means an agreeable companion. When they attempted to joke with him as to the young lady on the cliffs, he showed very plainly that he did not like it; and when Cornet Simpkinson after dinner raised his glass to drink a health to Miss O'Hara, Mr. Neville told him that he was an impertinent ass. It was then somewhat past nine, and it did not seem probable that the evening would go off pleasantly. Cornet Simpkinson lit his cigar, and tried to wink at the Captain. Neville stretched out his legs and pretended to go to sleep. At this moment it was a matter of intense regret to him that he had ever seen the West of Ireland.

At a little before ten Captain Johnstone retired, and the Cornet attempted an apology. He had not meant to say anything that Neville would not like. "It doesn't signify, my dear boy; only as a rule, never mention women's names," said Neville, speaking as though he were fully fitted by his experience to lay down the law on a matter so delicate. "Perhaps one hadn't better," said the Cornet, — and then that little difficulty was over. Cornet Simpkinson however thought of it all afterwards, and felt that that evening and that hour had been more important than any other evening or any other hour in his life.

At half-past ten, when Neville was beginning to think that he would take himself to bed, and was still cursing the evil star which had brought him to County Clare, there arose a clatter at the outside gate of the small barrack-yard. A man had posted all the way down from Limerick and desired to see Mr. Neville at once. The man had indeed come direct from Scroope, — by rail from Dublin to Limerick, and thence without delay on to Ennis. The Earl of Scroope was dead, and Frederic Neville was Earl of Scroope. The man brought a letter from Miss Mellerby, telling him the sad news and conjuring him in his aunt's name to come at once to the Manor. Of course he must start at once for the Manor. Of course he must attend as first mourner at his uncle's grave before he could assume his uncle's name and fortune.

In that first hour of his greatness the shock to him was not so great but that he at once thought of the O'Haras. He would leave Ennis the following morning at six, so as to catch the day mail train out of Limerick for Dublin. That was a necessity; but though so very short a span of time was left to him, he must still make arrangements about the O'Haras. He had hardly heard the news half an hour before he himself was knocking at the door of Mr. Crowe the attorney. He was admitted, and Mr. Crowe descended to him in a pair of slippers and a very old dressing-gown. Mr. Crowe, as he held his tallow candle up to his client's face, looked as if he didn't like it. "I know I must apologize," said Neville, "but

I have this moment received news of my uncle's death."

"The Earl?"

"Yes."

"And I have now the honour of — speaking to the Earl of Scroope."

"Never mind that. I must start for England almost immediately. I haven't above an hour or two. You must see that man, O'Hara, without me."

"Certainly, my lord."

"You shouldn't speak to me in that way yet," said Neville angrily. "You will be good enough to understand that the terms are fixed; — two hundred a year as long, as he remains in France and never molests anyone either by his presence or by letter. Thank you. I shall be so much obliged to you! I shall be back here after the funeral, and will arrange about payments. Good-night."

So it happened that Captain O'Hara had no opportunity on that occasion of seeing his proposed son-in-law. Mr. Crowe, fully crediting the power confided to him, did as he was bidden. He was very harsh to the poor Captain; but in such a condition a man can hardly expect that people should not be harsh to him. The Captain endeavoured to hold up his head, and to swagger, and to assume an air of pinchbeck respectability. But the attorney would not permit it. He required that the man should own himself to be penniless, a scoundrel, only anxious to be bought; and the Captain at last admitted the facts. The figure was the one thing important to him, — the figure and the nature of the assurance. Mr. Crowe had made his calculations, and put the matter very plainly. A certain number of francs, — a hundred francs, — would be paid to him weekly at any town in France he might select, — which however would be forfeited by any letter written either to Mrs. O'Hara, to Miss O'Hara, or to the Earl.

"The Earl!" ejaculated the Captain.

Mr. Crowe had been unable to refrain his tongue from the delicious title, but now corrected himself. "Nor Mr. Neville, I mean. No one will be bound to give you a farthing, and any letter asking for anything more will forfeit the allowance altogether." The Captain vainly endeavoured to make better terms, and of course accepted those proposed to him. He would live in Paris, — dear Paris. He took five pounds for his journey, and named an agent for the transmission of his money.

And so Fred Neville was the Earl of Scroope. He had still one other task to perform before he could make his journey home. He had to send tidings in some shape to Ardkill of what had happened. As he returned to the barracks from Mr. Crowe's residence he thought wholly of this. That other matter was now arranged. As one item of the cost of his adventure in County Clare he must pay two hundred a year to that reprobate, the Captain, as long as the reprobate chose to live, — and must also pay Mr. Crowe's bill for his assistance. This was a small matter to him as his wealth was now great, and he was not a man by nature much prone to think of money. Nevertheless it was a bad beginning of his life. Though he had declared himself to be quite indifferent on that head, he did feel that the arrangement was not altogether reputable, — that it was one which he could not explain to his own man of business without annoyance, and which might perhaps give him future trouble. Now he must prepare his message for the ladies at Ardkill, — especially to the lady whom on his last visit to the cottage he had found armed with a dagger for the reception of her husband. And as he returned back to the barracks it occurred to him that a messenger might be better than a letter. "Simpkinson," he said, going at once into the young man's bed-room, "have you heard what has happened to me?" Simpkinson had heard all about it, and expressed himself as "deucedly sorry" for the old man's death, but seemed to think that there might be consolation for that sorrow. "I must go to Scroope immediately," said Neville. "I have explained it all to Johnstone, and shall start almost at once. I shall first lie down and get an hour's sleep. I want you to do something for me." Simpkinson was devoted. Simpkinson would do anything. "I cut up a little rough just now when you mentioned Miss O'Hara's name." Simpkinson declared that he did not mind it in the least, and would never pronounce the name again as long as he lived. "But I want you to go and see her to-morrow," said Neville. Then Simpkinson sat bolt upright in bed.

Of course the youthful warrior undertook the commission. What youthful warrior would not go any distance to see a beautiful young lady on a cliff, and what youthful warrior would not undertake any journey to oblige a brother officer who was an Earl? Full instructions were at once given to him. He had better ask to see Mrs. O'Hara, — in describing whom Neville made no allusion to the dagger. He was told how to knock at the door, and send in word by the servant to say that he had called on behalf of Mr. Neville. He was to drive as far as Liscannor, and then get some boy to accompany him on foot as a guide. He would not perhaps mind walking two or three miles. Simpkinson declared that were it ten he would not mind it. He was then to tell Mrs. O'Hara — just the truth. He was to say that a messenger had come from Scroope announcing the death of the Earl, and that Neville had been obliged to start at once for England.

"But you will be back?" said Simpkinson.

Neville paused a moment. "Yes, I shall be back, but don't say anything of that to either of the ladies."

"Must I say I don't know? They'll be sure to ask, I should say."

"Of course they'll ask. Just tell them that the whole thing has been arranged so quickly that nothing has been settled, but that they shall hear from me at once. You can say that you suppose I shall be back, but that I promised that I would write. Indeed that will be the exact truth, as I don't at all know what I may do. Be as civil to them as possible."

"That's of course."

"They are ladies, you know."

"I supposed that."

"And I am most desirous to do all in my power to oblige them. You can say that I have arranged that other matter satisfactorily."

"That other matter?"

"They'll understand. The mother will at least, and you'd better say that to her. You'll go early."

"I'll start at seven if you like."

"Eight or nine will do. Thank you, Simpkinson. I'm so much obliged to you. I hope I shall see you over in England some day when things are a little settled." With this Simpkinson was delighted, — as he was also with the commission entrusted to him.

And so Fred Neville was the Earl of Scroope. Not that he owned even to himself that the title and all belonging to it were as yet in his own possession. Till the body of the old man should be placed in the family vault he would still be simply Fred Neville, a lieutenant in Her Majesty's 20th Hussars. As he travelled home to Scroope, to the old gloomy mansion which was now in truth not only his home, but his own house, to do just as he pleased with it, he had much to fill his mind. He was himself astonished to find with how great a weight his new dignities sat upon his shoulders, now that they were his own. But a few months since he had thought and even spoken of shifting them from himself to another, so that he might lightly enjoy a portion of the wealth which would belong to him without burdening himself with the duties of his position. He would take his yacht, and the girl he loved, and live abroad, with no present record of the coronet which would have descended to him, and with no assumption of the title. But already that feeling had died away within him. A few words spoken to him by the priest and a few serious thoughts within his own bosom had sufficed to explain to him that he must be the Earl of Scroope. The family honours had come to him, and he must support them, — either well or ill as his strength and principles might govern him. And he did understand that it was much to be a peer, an hereditary legislator, one who by the chance of his birth had a right to look for deferential respect even from his elders. It was much to be the lord of wide acres, the ruler of a large domain, the landlord of many tenants who would at any rate regard themselves as dependent on his goodness. It was much to be so placed that no consideration of money need be a bar to any wish, — that the considerations which should bar his pleasures need be only those of dignity, character, and propriety. His uncle had told him more than once how much a peer of England owed to his country and to his order; — how such a one is bound by no ordinary bonds to a life of high resolves, and good endeavours. "Sans reproche" was the motto of his house, and was emblazoned on the wall of the hall that was now his own. If it might be possible to him he would live up to it and neither degrade his order nor betray his country.

But as he thought of all this, he thought also of Kate O'Hara. With what difficulties had he surrounded the commencement of this life which he purposed to lead! How was he to escape from the mess of trouble which he had prepared for himself by his adventures in Ireland. An idea floated across his mind that very many men who stand in their natural manhood high in the world's esteem, have in their early youth formed ties such as that which now bound him to Kate O'Hara, — that they have been silly as he had been, and had then escaped from the effects of their folly without grievous damage. But yet he did not see his mode of escape. If money could do it for him he would make almost any sacrifice. If wealth and luxury could make his Kate happy, she should be happy as a Princess. But he did not believe either of her or of her mother that any money would be accepted as a sufficient atonement. And he hated himself for suggesting to himself that it might be possible. The girl was good, and had trusted him altogether. The mother was self-denying, devoted, and high-spirited. He knew that money would not suffice.

He need not return to Ireland unless he pleased. He could send over some agent to arrange his affairs, and allow the two women to break their hearts in their solitude upon the cliffs. Were he to do so he did not believe that they would follow him. They would write doubtless, but personally he might, probably, be quit of them in this fashion. But in this there would be a cowardice and a meanness which would make it impossible that he should ever again respect himself.

And thus he again entered Scroope, the lord and owner of all that he saw around him, — with by no means a happy heart or a light bosom.

Chapter VI.
The Earl of Scroope Is in Trouble.

Not a word was said to the young lord on his return home respecting the O'Haras till he himself had broached the subject. He found his brother Jack Neville at Scroope on his arrival, and Sophie Mellerby was still staying with his aunt. A day had been fixed for the funeral, but no one had ventured to make any other arrangement till the heir and owner should be there. He was received with solemn respect by the old servants who, as he observed, abstained from calling him by any name. They knew that it did not become them to transfer the former lord's title to the heir till all that remained of the former lord should be hidden from the world in the family vault; but they could not bring themselves to address a real Earl as Mr. Neville. His aunt was broken down by sorrow, but nevertheless, she treated him with a courtly deference. To her he was now the reigning sovereign among the Nevilles, and all Scroope and everything there was at his disposal. When he held her by the hand and spoke of her future life she only shook her head. "I am an old

217

woman, though not in years old as was my lord. But my life is done, and it matters not where I go."

"Dear aunt, do not speak of going. Where can you be so well as here?" But she only shook her head again and wept afresh. Of course it would not be fitting that she should remain in the house of the young Earl who was only her nephew by marriage. Scroope Manor would now become a house of joy, would be filled with the young and light of heart; there would be feasting there and dancing; horses neighing before the doors, throngs of carriages, new furniture, bright draperies, and perhaps, alas, loud revellings. It would not be fit that such a one as she should be at Scroope now that her lord had left her.

The funeral was an affair not of pomp but of great moment in those parts. Two or three Nevilles from other counties came to the house, as did also sundry relatives bearing other names. Mr. Mellerby was there, and one or two of the late Earl's oldest friends; but the great gathering was made up of the Scroope tenants, not one of whom failed to see his late landlord laid in his grave. "My Lord," said an old man to Fred, one who was himself a peer and was the young lord's cousin though they two had never met before, "My Lord," said the old man, as soon as they had returned from the grave, "you are called upon to succeed as good a man as ever it has been my lot to know. I loved him as a brother. I hope you will not lightly turn away from his example." Fred made some promise which at the moment he certainly intended to perform.

On the next morning the will was read. There was nothing in it, nor could there have been anything in it, which might materially affect the interests of the heir. The late lord's widow was empowered to take away from Scroope anything that she desired. In regard to money she was provided for so amply that money did not matter to her. A whole year's income from the estates was left to the heir in advance, so that he might not be driven to any momentary difficulty in assuming the responsibilities of his station. A comparatively small sum was left to Jack Neville, and a special gem to Sophie Mellerby. There were bequests to all the servants, a thousand pounds to the vicar of the parish, — which perhaps was the only legacy which astonished the legatee, — and his affectionate love to every tenant on the estate. All the world acknowledged that it was as good a will as the Earl could have made. Then the last of the strangers left the house, and the Earl of Scroope was left to begin his reign and do his duty as best he might.

Jack had promised to remain with him for a few days, and Sophie Mellerby, who had altogether given up her London season, was to stay with the widow till something should be settled as to a future residence. "If my aunt will only say that she will keep the house for a couple of years, she shall have it," said Fred to the young lady, — perhaps wishing to postpone for so long a time the embarrassment of the large domain; but to this Lady Scroope would not consent. If allowed she would remain till the end of July. By that time she would find herself a home.

"For the life of me, I don't know how to begin my life," said the new peer to his brother as they were walking about the park together.

"Do not think about beginning it at all. You won't be angry, and will know what I mean, when I say that you should avoid thinking too much of your own position."

"How am I to help thinking of it? It is so entirely changed from what it was."

"No Fred, — not entirely; nor as I hope, is it changed at all in those matters which are of most importance to you. A man's self, and his ideas of the manner in which he should rule himself, should be more to him than any outward accidents. Had that cousin of ours never died —"

"I almost wish he never had."

"It would then have been your ambition to live as an honourable gentleman. To be that now should be more to you than to be an Earl and a man of fortune."

"It's very easy to preach, Jack. You were always good at that. But here I am, and what am I to do? How am I to begin? Everybody says that I am to change nothing. The tenants will pay their rents, and Burnaby will look after things outside, and Mrs. Bunce will look after the things inside, and I may sit down and read a novel. When the gloom of my uncle's death has passed away, I suppose I shall buy a few more horses and perhaps begin to make a row about the pheasants. I don't know what else there is to do."

"You'll find that there are duties."

"I suppose I shall. Something is expected of me. I am to keep up the honour of the family; but it really seems to me that the best way of doing so would be to sit in my uncle's arm chair and go to sleep as he did."

"As a first step in doing something you should get a wife for yourself. If once you had a settled home, things would arrange themselves round you very easily."

"Ah, yes; — a wife. You know, Jack, I told you about that girl in County Clare."

"You must let nothing of that kind stand in your way."

"Those are your ideas of high moral grandeur! Just now my own personal conduct was to be all in all to me, and the rank nothing. Now I am to desert a girl I love because I am an English peer."

"What has passed between you and the young lady, of course I do not know."

"I may as well tell you the whole truth," said Fred. And he told it. He told it honestly, — almost honestly. It is very hard for a man to tell a story truly against himself, but he intended to tell the whole truth. "Now what must I do? Would you have me marry her?" Jack Neville paused for a long time. "At any rate you can say yes, or no."

"It is very hard to say yes, or no."

"I can marry no one else. I can see my way so far. You had better tell Sophie Mellerby everything, and then a son of yours shall be the future Earl."

"We are both of us young as yet, Fred, and need not think of that. If you do mean to marry Miss O'Hara you should lose not a day; — not a day."

"But what if I don't. You are always very ready with advice, but you have given me none as yet."

"How can I advise you? I should have heard the very words in which you made your promise before I could dare to say whether it should be kept or broken. As a rule a man should keep his word."

"Let the consequences be what they may?"

"A man should keep his word certainly. And I know no promise so solemn as that made to a woman when followed by conduct such as yours has been."

"And what will people say then as to my conduct to the family? How will they look on me when I bring home the daughter of that scoundrel?"

"You should have thought of that before."

"But I was not told. Do you not see that I was deceived there. Mrs. O'Hara clearly said that the man was dead. And she told me nothing of the galleys."

"How could she tell you that?"

"But if she has deceived me, how can I be

expected to keep my promise? I love the girl dearly. If I could change places with you, I would do so this very minute, and take her away with me, and she should certainly be my wife. If it were only myself, I would give up all to her. I would, by heaven. But I cannot sacrifice the family. As to solemn promises, did I not swear to my uncle that I would not disgrace the family by such a marriage? Almost the last word that I spoke to him was that. Am I to be untrue to him? There are times in which it seems impossible that a man should do right."

"There are times in which a man may be too blind to see the right," said Jack, — sparing his brother in that he did not remind him that those dilemmas always come from original wrong-doing.

"I think I am resolved not to marry her," said Fred.

"If I were in your place I think I should marry her," said Jack; — "but I will not speak with certainty even of myself."

"I shall not. But I will be true to her all the same. You may be sure that I shall not marry at all." Then he recurred to his old scheme. "If I can find any mode of marrying her in some foreign country, so that her son and mine shall not be the legitimate heir to the title and estates, I would go there at once with her, though it were to the further end of the world. You can understand now what I mean when I say that I do not know how to begin." Jack acknowledged that in that matter he did understand his brother. It is always hard for a man to commence any new duty when he knows that he has a millstone round his neck which will probably make that duty impracticable at last.

He went on with his life at Scroope for a week after the funeral without resolving upon anything, or taking any steps towards solving the O'Hara difficulty. He did ride about among the tenants, and gave some trifling orders as to the house and stables. His brother was still with him, and Miss Mellerby remained at the Manor. But he knew that the thunder-cloud must break over his head before long, and at last the storm was commenced. The first drops fell upon him in the soft form of a letter from Kate O'Hara.

DEAREST FRED,

I am not quite sure that I ought to address you like that; but I always shall unless you tell me not. We have been expecting a letter from you every day since you went. Your friend from Ennis came here, and brought us the news of your uncle's death. We were very sorry; at least I was certainly. I liked to think of you a great deal better as my own Fred, than as a great lord. But you will still be my own Fred always; will you not?

Mother said at once that it was a matter of course that you should go to England; but your friend, whose name we never heard, said that you had sent him especially to promise that you would write quite immediately, and that you would come back very soon. I do not know what he will think of me, because I asked him whether he was quite, quite sure that you would come back. If he thinks that I love you better than my own soul, he only thinks the truth.

Pray, — pray write at once. Mother is getting vexed because there is no letter. I am never vexed with my own darling love, but I do so long for a letter. If you knew how I felt, I do think you would write almost every day, — if it were only just one short word. If you would say, 'Dear Love,' that would be enough. And pray come. Oh do, do, pray come! Cannot you think how I must long to see you! The gentleman who came here said that you would come, and I know you will. But pray come soon. Think, now, how you are all the world to me. You are more than all the world to me.

I am not ill as I was when you were here. But I never go outside the door now. I never shall go outside the door again till you come. I don't care now for going out upon the rocks. I don't care even for the birds as you are not here to watch them with me. I sit with the skin of the seal you gave me behind my head, and I pretend to sleep. But though I am quite still for hours I am not asleep, but thinking always of you.

We have neither seen or heard anything

more of my father, and Father Marty says that you have managed about that very generously. You are always generous and good. I was so wretched all that day, that I thought I should have died. You will not think ill of your Kate, will you, because her father is bad?

Pray write when you get this, and above all things let us know when you will come to us.

Always, always, and always,
Your own
KATE.

Two days after this, while the letter was still unanswered, there came another from Mrs. O'Hara which was, if possible, more grievous to him than that from her daughter.

"My Lord," the letter began. When he read this he turned from it with a sickening feeling of disgust. Of course the woman knew that he was now Earl of Scroope; but it would have been so desirable that there should have been no intercourse between her and him except under the name by which she had hitherto known him. And then in the appellation as she used it there seemed to be a determination to reproach him which must, he knew, lead to great misery.

MY LORD,

The messenger you sent to us brought us good news, and told us that you were gone home to your own affairs. That I suppose was right, but why have you not written to us before this? Why have you not told my poor girl that you will come to her, and atone to her for the injury you have done in the only manner now possible? I cannot and do not believe that you intend to evade the solemn promises that you have made her, and allow her to remain here a ruined outcast, and the mother of your child. I have thought you to be both a gentleman and a christian, and I still think so. Most assuredly you would be neither were you disposed to leave her desolate, while you are in prosperity.

I call upon you, my lord, in the most solemn manner, with all the energy and anxiety of a mother, — of one who will be of all women the most broken-hearted if you wrong her, — to write at once and let me know when you will be here to keep your promise. For the sake of your own offspring I implore you not to delay.

We feel under deep obligations to you for what you did in respect of that unhappy man. We have never for a moment doubted your generosity.

Yours, My Lord,
With warmest affection, if you will admit it,
C. O'HARA.

P.S. I ask you to come at once and keep your word. Were you to think of breaking it, I would follow you through the world.

The young Earl, when he received this, was not at a loss for a moment to attribute the body of Mrs. O'Hara's letter to Father Marty's power of composition, and the postscript to the unaided effort of the lady herself. Take it as he might — as coming from Mrs. O'Hara or from the priest, — he found the letter to be a great burden to him. He had not as yet answered the one received from Kate, as to the genuineness of which he had entertained no doubt. How should he answer such letters? Some answer must of course be sent, and must be the forerunner of his future conduct. But how should he write his letter when he had not as yet resolved what his conduct should be?

He did attempt to write a letter, not to either of the ladies, but to the priest, explaining that in the ordinary sense of the word he could not and would not marry Miss O'Hara, but that in any way short of that legitimate and usual mode of marriage, he would bind himself to her, and that when so bound he would be true to her for life. He would make any settlement that he, Father Marty, might think right either upon the mother or upon the daughter. But Countess of Scroope the daughter of that Captain O'Hara should not become through his means. Then he endeavoured to explain the obligation laid upon him by his uncle, and the excuse which he thought he could plead in not having been informed of Captain O'Hara's existence. But the letter when written seemed to him to be poor and mean, cringing and at the same time false. He told himself that it would not suffice. It was manifest to him that he must go back to County Clare, even though he should encounter Mrs. O'Hara, dagger in hand. What was any personal danger to himself in such an affair as this? And if he did not fear a woman's dagger, was he to fear a woman's tongue, — or the tongue of a priest? So he tore the letter, and resolved that he would write and name a day on which he would appear at Ardkill. At any rate such a letter as that might be easily written, and might be made soft with words of love.

DEAREST KATE,

I will be with you on the 15th or on the 16th at latest. You should remember that a man has a good deal to do and think of when he gets pitchforked into such a new phase of life as mine. Do not, however, think that I quarrel with you, my darling. That I will never do. My love to your mother.

Ever your own,
FRED.

I hate signing the other name.

This letter was not only written but sent.

CHAPTER VII.
SANS REPROCHE.

Three or four days after writing his letter to Kate O'Hara, the Earl told his aunt that he must return to Ireland, and he named the day on which he would leave Scroope. "I did not think that you would go back there," she said. He could see by the look of her face and by the anxious glance of her eye that she had in her heart the fear of Kate O'Hara, — as he had also.

"I must return. I came away at a moment's notice."

"But you have written about leaving the regiment."

"Yes; — I have done that. In the peculiar circumstances I don't suppose they will want me to serve again. Indeed I've had a letter, just a private note, from one of the fellows at the Horse Guards explaining all that."

"I don't see why you should go at all; — indeed I do not."

"What am I to do about my things? I owe some money. I've got three or four horses there. My very clothes are all about just as I left them when I came away."

"Any body can manage all that. Give the horses away."

"I had rather not give away my horses," he said laughing. "The fact is I must go." She could urge nothing more to him on that occasion. She did not then mention the existence of Kate O'Hara. But he knew well that she was thinking of the girl, and he knew also that the activity of Lady Mary Quin had not slackened. But his aunt, he thought, was more afraid of him now that he was the Earl than she had been when he was only the heir; and it might be that this feeling would save him from the mention of Kate O'Hara's name.

To some extent the dowager was afraid of her nephew. She knew at least that the young man was all-powerful and might act altogether as he listed. In whatever she might say she could not now be supported by the authority of the Lord of Scroope. He himself was lord of Scroope; and were he to tell her simply to hold her tongue and mind her own business she could only submit. But she was not the woman to allow any sense of fear, or any solicitude as to the respect due to herself, to stand in the way of the performance of a duty. It may be declared on her behalf that had it been in her nephew's power to order her head off in punishment for her interference, she would still have spoken had she conceived it to be right to speak.

But within her own bosom there had been dreadful conflicts as to that duty. Lady Mary

Quin had by no means slackened her activity. Lady Mary Quin had learned the exact condition of Kate O'Hara, and had sent the news to her friend with greedy rapidity. And in sending it Lady Mary Quin entertained no slightest doubt as to the duty of the present Earl of Scroope. According to her thinking it could not be the duty of an Earl of Scroope in any circumstances to marry a Kate O'Hara. There are women, who in regard to such troubles as now existed at Ardkill cottage, always think that the woman should be punished as the sinner and that the man should be assisted to escape. The hardness of heart of such women, — who in all other views of life are perhaps tender and soft-natured, — is one of the marvels of our social system. It is as though a certain line were drawn to include all women, — a line, but, alas, little more than a line, — by overstepping which, or rather by being known to have overstepped it, a woman ceases to be a woman in the estimation of her own sex. That the existence of this feeling has strong effect in saving women from passing the line, none of us can doubt. That its general tendency may be good rather than evil, is possible. But the hardness necessary to preserve the rule, a hardness which must be exclusively feminine but which is seldom wanting, is a marvellous feature in the female character. Lady Mary Quin probably thought but little on the subject. The women in the cottage on the cliff, who were befriended by Father Marty, were to her dangerous scheming Roman Catholic adventurers. The proper triumph of Protestant virtue required that they should fail in their adventures. She had always known that there would be something disreputable heard of them sooner or later. When the wretched Captain came into the neighbourhood, — and she soon heard of his coming, — she was gratified by feeling that her convictions had been correct. When the sad tidings as to poor Kate reached her ears, she had "known that it would be so." That such a girl should be made Countess of Scroope in reward for her wickedness would be to her an event horrible, almost contrary to Divine Providence, — a testimony that the Evil One was being allowed peculiar power at the moment, and would no doubt have been used in her own circles to show the ruin that had been brought upon the country by Catholic emancipation. She did not for a moment doubt that the present Earl should be encouraged to break any promises of marriage to the making of which he might have been allured.

But it was not so with Lady Scroope. She, indeed, came to the same conclusion as her friend, but she did so with much difficulty and after many inward struggles. She understood and valued the customs of the magic line. In her heart of hearts she approved of a different code of morals for men and women. That which merited instant, and as regarded this world, perpetual condemnation in a woman, might in a man be very easily forgiven. A sigh, a shake of the head, and some small innocent stratagem that might lead to a happy marriage and settlement in life with increased income, would have been her treatment of such sin for the heirs of the great and wealthy. She knew that the world could not afford to ostracise the men, — though happily it might condemn the women. Nevertheless, when she came to the single separated instance, though her heart melted with no ruth for the woman, — in such cases the woman must be seen before the ruth is felt, — though pity for Kate O'Hara did not influence her, she did acknowledge the sanctity of a gentleman's word. If, as Lady Mary told her, and as she could so well believe, the present Earl of Scroope had given to this girl a promise that he would marry her, if he had bound himself by his pledged word, as a nobleman and a gentleman, how could she bid him become a perjured knave? Sans reproche! Was he thus to begin to live and to deserve the motto of his house by the conduct of his life?

But then the evil that would be done was so great! She did not for a moment doubt all that Lady Mary told her about the girl. The worst of it had indeed been admitted. She was a Roman Catholic, ill-born, ill-connected, damaged utterly by a parent so low that nothing lower could possibly be raked out of the world's gutters. And now the girl herself was — a castaway. Such a marriage as that of which Lady Mary spoke would not only injure the house of Scroope for the present generation, but would tend to its final downfall. Would it not be known throughout all England that the next Earl of Scroope would be the grandson of a convict? Might there not be questions as to the legitimacy of the assumed heir? She herself knew of noble families which had been scattered, confounded, and almost ruined by such imprudence. Hitherto the family of Scroope had been continued from generation to generation without stain, — almost without stain. It had felt it to be a fortunate thing that the late heir had died because of the pollution of his wretched marriage. And now must evil as bad befall it, worse evil perhaps, through the folly of this young man? Must that proud motto be taken down from its place in the hall from very shame? But the evil had not been done yet, and it might be that her words could save the house from ruin and disgrace.

She was a woman of whom it may be said that whatever difficulty she might have in deciding a question she could recognise the necessity of a decision and could abide by it when she had made it. It was with great difficulty that she could bring herself to think that an Earl of Scroope should be false to a promise by which he had seduced a woman, but she did succeed in bringing herself to such thought. Her very heart bled within her as she acknowledged the necessity. A lie to her was abominable. A lie, to be told by herself, would have been hideous to her. A lie to be told by him, was worse. As virtue, what she called virtue, was the one thing indispensable to women, so was truth the one thing indispensable to men. And yet she must tell him to lie, and having resolved so to tell him, must use all her intellect to defend the lie, — and to insist upon it.

He was determined to return to Ireland, and there was nothing that she could do to prevent his return. She could not bid him shun a danger simply because it was a danger. He was his own master, and were she to do so he would only laugh at her. Of authority with him she had none. If she spoke, he must listen. Her position would secure so much to her from courtesy, — and were she to speak of the duty which he owed to his name and to the family he could hardly laugh. She therefore sent to him a message. Would he kindly go to her in her own room? Of course he attended to her wishes and went. "You mean to leave us to-morrow, Fred," she said. We all know the peculiar solemnity of a widow's dress, — the look of self-sacrifice on the part of the woman which the dress creates; and have perhaps recognised the fact that if the woman be deterred by no necessities of œconomy in her toilet, — as in such material circumstances the splendour is more perfect if splendour be the object, — so also is the self-sacrifice more abject. And with this widow an appearance of melancholy solemnity, almost of woe, was natural to her. She was one whose life had ever been serious, solemn, and sad. Wealth and the outward pomp of circumstances had conferred upon her a certain dignity; and with that doubtless there had reached her some feeling of satisfaction. Religion too had given her comfort, and a routine of small duties had saved her from the wretchedness of ennui. But life with her had had no laughter, and had seldom smiled. Now in the first days of her widowhood she regarded her course as run, and looked upon herself as one who, in speaking, almost spoke from the tomb. All this had its effect upon the young lord. She did inspire him with a certain awe; and though her weeds gave her no authority, they did give her weight.

"Yes; I shall start to-morrow," he replied.

"And you still mean to go to Ireland?"

"Yes; — I must go to Ireland. I shan't stay there, you know."

Then she paused a moment before she proceeded. "Shall you see — that young woman when you are there?"

"I suppose I shall see her."

"Pray do not think that I desire to interfere with your private affairs. I know well that I have no right to assume over you any of that affectionate authority which a mother might have, — though in truth I love you as a son."

"I would treat you just as I would my own mother."

"No, Fred; that cannot be so. A mother would throw her arms round you and cling to you if she saw you going into danger. A mother would follow you, hoping that she might save you."

"But there is no danger."

"Ah, Fred, I fear there is."

"What danger?"

"You are now the head of one of the oldest and the noblest families in this which in my heart I believe to be the least sinful among the sinful nations of the wicked world."

"I don't quite know how that may be; — I mean about the world. Of course I understand about the family."

"But you love your country?"

"Oh yes. I don't think there's any place like England, — to live in."

"And England is what it is because there are still some left among us who are born to high rank and who know how to live up to the standard that is required of them. If ever there was such a man, your uncle was such a one."

"I'm sure he was; — just what he ought to have been."

"Honourable, true, affectionate, self-denying, affable to all men, but ever conscious of his rank, giving much because much had been given to him, asserting his nobility for the benefit of those around him, proud of his order for the sake of his country, bearing his sorrows with the dignity of silence, a nobleman all over, living on to the end sans reproche! He was a man whom you may dare to imitate, though to follow him may be difficult." She spoke not loudly, but clearly,

238

looking him full in the face as she stood motionless before him.

"He was all that," said Fred, almost overpowered by the sincere solemnity of his aunt's manner.

"Will you try to walk in his footsteps?"

"Two men can never be like one another in that way. I shall never be what he was. But I'll endeavour to get along as well as I can."

"You will remember your order?"

"Yes, I will. I do remember it. Mind you, aunt, I am not glad that I belong to it. I think I do understand about it all, and will do my best. But Jack would have made a better Earl than I shall do. That's the truth."

"The Lord God has placed you, — and you must pray to Him that He will enable you to do your duty in that state of life to which it has pleased Him to call you. You are here and must bear his decree; and whether it be a privilege to enjoy, you must enjoy it, or a burden to bear, you must endure it."

"It is so of course."

"Knowing that, you must know also how incumbent it is upon you not to defile the stock from which you are sprung."

"I suppose it has been defiled," said Fred, who had been looking into the history of the family. "The ninth Earl seems to have married nobody knows whom. And his son was my uncle's grandfather."

This was a blow to Lady Scroope, but she bore

it with dignity and courage. "You would hardly wish it to be said that you had copied the only one of your ancestors who did amiss. The world was rougher then than it is now, and he of whom you speak was a soldier."

"I'm a soldier too," said the Earl.

"Oh, Fred, is it thus you answer me! He was a soldier in rough times, when there were wars. I think he married when he was with the army under Marlborough."

"I have not seen anything of that kind, certainly."

"Your country is at peace, and your place is here, among your tenantry, at Scroope. You will promise me, Fred, that you will not marry this girl in Ireland?"

"If I do, the fault will be all with that old maid at Castle Quin."

"Do not say that, Fred. It is impossible. Let her conduct have been what it may, it cannot make that right in you which would have been wrong, or that wrong which would have been right."

"She's a nasty meddlesome cat."

"I will not talk about her. What good would it do? You cannot at any rate be surprised at my extreme anxiety. You did promise your uncle most solemnly that you would never marry this young lady."

"If I did, that ought to be enough." He was now waxing angry and his face was becoming red. He would bear a good deal from his uncle's widow, but he felt his own power and was not prepared to bear much more.

"Of course I cannot bind you. I know well how impotent I am, — how powerless to exercise control. But I think, Fred, that for your uncle's sake you will not refuse to repeat your promise to me, if you intend to keep it. Why is it that I am so anxious? It is for your sake, and for the sake of a name which should be dearer to you than it is even to me."

"I have no intention of marrying at all."

"Do not say that."

"I do say it. I do not want to keep either you or Jack in the dark as to my future life. This young lady, — of whom, by the by, neither you nor Lady Mary Quin know anything, shall not become Countess of Scroope. To that I have made up my mind."

"Thank God."

"But as long as she lives I will make no woman Countess of Scroope. Let Jack marry this girl that he is in love with. They shall live here and have the house to themselves if they like it. He will look after the property and shall have whatever income old Mellerby thinks proper. I will keep the promise I made to my uncle, — but the keeping of it will make it impossible for me to live here. I would prefer now that you should say no more on the subject." Then he left her, quitting the room with some stateliness in his step, as though conscious that at such a moment as this it behoved him to assume his rank.

The dowager sat alone all that morning thinking of the thing she had done. She did now believe that he was positively resolved not to marry Kate O'Hara, and she believed also that she herself had fixed him in that resolution. In doing so had she or had she not committed a deadly sin? She knew almost with accuracy what had occurred on the coast of Clare. A young girl, innocent herself up to that moment, had been enticed to her ruin by words of love which had been hallowed in her ears by vows of marriage. Those vows which had possessed so deadly an efficacy, were now to be simply broken! The cruelty to her would be damnable, devilish, — surely worthy of hell if any sin of man can be so called! And she, who could not divest herself of a certain pride taken in the austere morality of her own life, she who was now a widow anxious to devote her life solely to God, had persuaded the man to this sin, in order that her successor as Countess of Scroope might not be, in her opinion, unfitting for nobility! The young lord had promised her that he would be guilty of this sin, so damnable, so devilish, telling her as he did so, that as a consequence of his promise he must continue to live a life of wickedness! In the agony of her spirit she threw herself upon her knees and implored the Lord to pardon her and to guide her. But even while kneeling before the throne of heaven she could not drive the pride of birth out of her heart. That the young Earl might be saved from the damning sin and also from the polluting marriage; — that was the prayer she prayed.

Chapter VIII.
Loose about the World.

The Countess was seen no more on that day, — was no more seen at least by either of the two brothers. Miss Mellerby was with her now and again, but on each occasion only for a few minutes, and reported that Lady Scroope was ill and could not appear at dinner. She would, however, see her nephew before he started on the following morning.

Fred himself was much affected by the interview with his aunt. No doubt he had made a former promise to his uncle, similar to that which had now been exacted from him. No doubt he had himself resolved, after what he had thought to be mature consideration that he would not marry the girl, justifying to himself this decision by the deceit which he thought had been practised upon him in regard to Captain O'Hara. Nevertheless, he felt that by what had now occurred he was bound more strongly against the marriage than he had ever been bound before. His promise to his uncle might have been regarded as being obligatory only as long as his uncle lived. His own decision he would have been at liberty to change when he pleased to do so. But, though his aunt was almost nothing to him, — was not in very truth his aunt, but only the widow of his uncle, there had been a solemnity about the engagement as he had now made it with her, which he felt to be definitely binding. He must go to Ardkill prepared to tell them absolutely the truth. He would make any arrangement they pleased as to their future joint lives, so long as it was an arrangement by which Kate should not become Countess of Scroope. He did not attempt to conceal from himself the dreadful nature of the task before him. He knew what would be the indignation of the priest. He could picture to himself the ferocity of the mother, defending her young as a lioness would her whelp. He could imagine that that dagger might again be brought from its hiding place. And, worse than all, he would see the girl prostrate in her woe, and appealing to his love and to his oaths, when the truth as to her future life should be revealed to her. But yet he did not think of shunning the task before him. He could not endure to live a coward in his own esteem.

He was unlike himself and very melancholy. "It has been so good of you to remain here," he said to Sophie Mellerby. They had now become intimate and almost attached to each other as friends. If she had allowed a spark of hope to become bright within her heart in regard to the young Earl that had long since been quenched.

She had acknowledged to herself that had it been possible in other respects they would not have suited each other, — and now they were friends.

"I love your aunt dearly and have been very glad to be with her."

"I wish you would learn to love somebody else dearly."

"Perhaps I shall, some day, — somebody else; though I don't at all know who it may be."

"You knew whom I mean."

"I suppose I do."

"And why not love him? Isn't he a good fellow?"

"One can't love all the good fellows, Lord Scroope."

"You'll never find a better one than he is."

"Did he commission you to speak for him?"

"You know he didn't. You know that he would be the last man in the world to do so?"

"I was surprised."

"But I had a reason for speaking."

"No doubt."

"I don't suppose it will have any effect with you; — but it is something you ought to know. If any man of my age can be supposed to have made up his mind on such a matter, you may believe that I have made up my mind that I will — never marry."

"What nonsense, Lord Scroope."

"Well; — yes; perhaps it is. But I am so convinced of it myself that I shall ask my brother to come and live here — permanently, — as master of the place. As he would have to leave his regiment it would of course be necessary that his position here should be settled, — and it shall be settled."

"I most sincerely hope that you will always live here yourself."

"It won't suit me. Circumstances have made it impossible. If he will not do so, nor my aunt, the house must be shut up. I am most anxious that this should not be done. I shall implore him to remain here, and to be here exactly as I should have been, — had things with me not have been so very unfortunate. He will at any rate have a house to offer you, if —"

"Lord Scroope!"

"I know what you are going to say, Sophie."

"I don't know that I am as yet disposed to marry for the sake of a house to shelter me."

"Of course you would say that; but still I think that I have been right to tell you. I am sure you will believe my assurance that Jack knows nothing of all this."

That same evening he said nearly the same thing to his brother, though in doing so he made no special allusion to Sophie Mellerby. "I know that there is a great deal that a fellow should do, living in such a house as this, but I am not the man to do it. It's a very good kind of life, if you happen to be up to it. I am not, but you are."

"My dear Fred, you can't change the accidents of birth."

"In a great measure I can; or at least we can

do so between us. You can't be Lord Scroope, but you can be master of Scroope Manor."

"No I can't; — and, which is more, I won't. Don't think I am uncivil."

"You are uncivil, Jack."

"At any rate I am not ungrateful. I only want you to understand thoroughly that such an arrangement is out of the question. In no condition of life would I care to be the locum tenens for another man. You are now five or six and twenty. At thirty you may be a married man with an absolute need for your own house."

"I would execute any deed."

"So that I might be enabled to keep the owner of the property out of the only place that is fit for him! It is a power which I should not use, and do not wish to possess. Believe me, Fred, that a man is bound to submit himself to the circumstances by which he is surrounded, when it is clear that they are beneficial to the world at large. There must be an Earl of Scroope, and you at present are the man."

They were sitting together out upon the terrace after dinner, and for a time there was silence. His brother's arguments were too strong for the young lord, and it was out of his power to deal with one so dogmatic. But he did not forget the last words that had been spoken. It may be that "I shall not be the man very long," he said at last.

"Any of us may die to-day or to-morrow," said Jack.

"I have a kind of presentiment, — not that I shall die, but that I shall never see Scroope again. It seems as though I were certainly leaving for ever a place that has always been distasteful to me."

"I never believe anything of presentiments."

"No; of course not. You're not that sort of fellow at all. But I am. I can't think of myself as living here with a dozen old fogies about the place all doing nothing, touching their hats, my-lording me at every turn, looking respectable, but as idle as pickpockets."

"You'll have to do it."

"Perhaps I shall, but I don't think it." Then there was again silence for a time. "The less said about it the better, but I know that I've got a very difficult job before me in Ireland."

"I don't envy you, Fred; — not that."

"It is no use talking about it. It has got to be done, and the sooner done the better. What I shall do when it is done, I have not the most remote idea. Where I shall be living this day month I cannot guess. I can only say one thing certainly, and that is that I shall not come back here. There never was a fellow so loose about the world as I am."

It was terrible that a young man who had it in his power to do so much good or so much evil should have had nothing to bind him to the better course! There was the motto of his house, and the promises which he had made to his uncle persuading him to that which was respectable and as he thought dull; and opposed to those influences there was an unconquerable feeling on his own part that he was altogether unfitted for the kind of life that was expected of him. Joined to this there was the fact of that unfortunate connection in Ireland from which he knew that it would be base to fly, and which, as it seemed to him, made any attempt at respectability impossible to him.

Early on the following morning, as he was preparing to start, his aunt again sent for him. She came out to him in the sitting-room adjoining her bedroom and there embraced him. Her eyes were red with weeping, and her face wan with care. "Fred," she said; "dear Fred."

"Good-bye, aunt. The last word I have to say is that I implore you not to leave Scroope as long as you are comfortable here."

"You will come back?"

"I cannot say anything certain about that."

She still had hold of him with both hands and was looking into his face with loving, frightened, wistful eyes. "I know," she said, "that you will be thinking of what passed between us yesterday."

"Certainly I shall remember it."

"I have been praying for you, Fred; and now I tell you to look to your Father which is in Heaven for guidance, and not to take it from any poor frail sinful human being. Ask Him to keep your feet steady in the path, and your heart pure, and your thoughts free from wickedness. Oh, Fred, keep your mind and body clear before

Him, and if you will kneel to Him for protection, He will show you a way through all difficulties." It was thus that she intended to tell him that his promise to her, made on the previous day, was to count for nought, and that he was to marry the girl if by no other way he could release himself from vice. But she could not bring herself to declare to him in plain terms that he had better marry Kate O'Hara, and bring his new Countess to Scroope in order that she might be fitly received by her predecessor. It might be that the Lord would still show him a way out of the two evils.

But his brother was more clear of purpose with him, as they walked together out to the yard in which the young Earl was to get into his carriage. "Upon the whole, Fred, if I were you I should marry that girl." This he said quite abruptly. The young lord shook his head. "It may be that I do not know all the circumstances. If they be as I have heard them from you, I should marry her. Good-bye. Let me hear from you, when you have settled as to going anywhere."

"I shall be sure to write," said Fred as he took the reins and seated him in the phaeton.

His brother's advice he understood plainly, and that of his aunt he thought that he understood. But he shook his head again as he told himself that he could not now be guided by either of them.

CHAPTER IX.
AT LISCANNOR.

The young lord slept one night at Ennis, and on the third morning after his departure from Scroope, started in his gig for Liscannor and the cliffs of Moher. He took a servant with him and a change of clothes. And as he went his heart was very heavy. He could not live a coward in his own esteem. Were it not so how willingly would he have saved himself from the misery of this journey, and have sent to his Kate to bid her come to him in England! He feared the priest, and he feared his Kate's mother; — not her dagger, but her eyes and scorching words. He altogether doubted his own powers to perform satisfactorily the task before him. He knew men who could do it. His brother Jack would do it, were it possible that his brother Jack should be in such a position. But for himself, he was conscious of a softness of heart, a feminine tenderness, which, — to do him justice, — he did not mistake for sincerity, that rendered him unfit for the task before him. The farther he journeyed from Scroope and the nearer that he found himself to the cliffs the stronger did the feeling grow within him, till it had become almost tragical in its dominion over him. But still he went on. It was incumbent on him to pay one more visit to the cliffs and he journeyed on.

At Limerick he did not even visit the barracks to see his late companions of the regiment. At Ennis he slept in his old room, and of course the two officers who were quartered there came to him. But they both declared when they left him that the Earl of Scroope and Fred Neville were very different persons, attributing the difference solely to the rank and wealth of the new peer. Poor Simpkinson had expected long whispered confidential conversations respecting the ladies of Ardkill; but the Earl had barely thanked him for his journey; and the whispered confidence, which would have been so delightful, was at once impossible. "By Heaven, there's nothing like rank to spoil a fellow. He was a good fellow once." So spoke Captain Johnstone, as the two officers retreated together from the Earl's room.

And the Earl also saw Mr. Crowe the attorney. Mr. Crowe recognized at its full weight the importance of a man whom he might now call "My Lord" as often as he pleased, and as to whose pecuniary position he had made some gratifying inquiries. A very few words sufficed. Captain O'Hara had taken his departure, and the money would be paid regularly. Mr. Crowe also noticed the stern silence of the man, but thought that it was becoming in an Earl with so truly noble a property. Of the Castle Quin people who could hardly do more than pay their way like country gentlefolk, and who were mere Irish, Mr. Crowe did not think much.

Every hour that brought the lord nearer to Liscannor added a weight to his bosom. As he drove his gig along the bleak road to Ennistimon his heart was very heavy indeed. At Maurice's mills, the only resting-place on the road, it had been his custom to give his horse a mouthful of water; but he would not do so now though the poor beast would fain have stopped there. He drove the animal on ruthlessly, himself driven by a feeling of unrest which would not allow him to pause. He hated the country now, and almost told himself that he hated all whom it contained. How miserable was his lot, that he should have bound himself in the opening of his splendour, in the first days of a career that might have been so splendid, to misfortune that was squalid and mean as this. To him, to one placed by circumstances as he was placed, it was squalid and mean. By a few soft words spoken to a poor girl whom he had chanced to find among the rocks he had so bound himself with vile manacles, had so crippled, hampered and fettered himself, that he was forced to renounce all the glories of his station. Wealth almost unlimited was at his command, — and rank, and youth, and such personal gifts of appearance and disposition as best serve to win general love. He had talked to his brother of his unfitness for his earldom; but he could have blazoned it forth at Scroope and up in London, with the best of young lords, and have loved well to do so. But this adventure, as he had been wont to call it, had fallen upon him, and had broken him as it were in pieces. Thousands a year he would have paid to be rid of his adventure; but thousands a year, he knew well, were of no avail. He might have sent over some English Mr. Crowe with offers almost royal; but he had been able so to discern the persons concerned as to know that royal offers, of which the royalty would be simply money royalty, could be of no avail. How would that woman have looked at any messenger who had come to her with offers of money, — and proposed to take her child into some luxurious but disgraceful seclusion? And in what language would Father Marty have expressed himself on such a proposed arrangement? And so the Earl of Scroope drove on with his heart falling ever lower and lower within his bosom.

It had of course been necessary that he should form some plan. He proposed to get rooms for one night at the little inn at Ennistimon, to leave his gig there, and then to take one of the country cars on to Liscannor. It would, he thought, be best to see the priest first. Let him look at his task which way he would, he found that every part of it was bad. An interview with Father Marty would be very bad, for he must declare his intentions in such a way that no doubt respecting them must be left on the priest's mind. He would speak only to three persons; — but to all those three he must now tell the certain truth. There were causes at work which made it impossible that Kate O'Hara should become Countess of Scroope. They might tear him to pieces, but from that decision he would not budge. Subject to that decision they might do with him and with all that belonged to him almost as they pleased. He would explain this first to the priest if it should chance that he found the priest at home.

He left his gig and servant at Ennistimon and proceeded as he had intended along the road to Liscannor on an outside car. In the mid-distance about two miles out of the town he met Father Marty riding on the road. He had almost hoped, — nay, he had hoped, — that the priest might not be at home. But here was the lion in his path. "Ah, my Lord," said the priest in his sweetest tone of good humour, — and his tones when he was so disposed were very sweet, — "Ah, my Lord, this is a sight good for sore eyes. They tould me you were to be here to-day or to-morrow, and I took it for granted therefore it'd be the day afther. But you're as good as the best of your word." The Earl of Scroope got off the car, and holding the priest's hand, answered the kindly salutation. But he did so with a constrained air and with a solemnity which the priest also attributed to his newly-begotten rank. Fred Neville, — as he had been a week or two since, — was almost grovelling in the dust before the priest's eyes; but the priest for the moment thought that he was wrapping himself up in the sables and ermine of his nobility. However, he had come back, — which was more perhaps than Father Marty had expected, — and the best must be made of him with reference to poor Kate's future happiness. "You're going on to Ardkill, I suppose, my Lord," he said.

"Yes; — certainly; but I intended to take the Liscannor road on purpose to see you. I shall leave the car at Liscannor and walk up. You could not return, I suppose?"

"Well, — yes, — I might."

"If you could, Father Marty —"

"Oh, certainly." The priest now saw that there was something more in the man's manner than lordly pride. As the Earl got again up on his car, the priest turned his horse, and the two travelled back through the village without further conversation. The priest's horse was given up to the boy in the yard, and he then led the way into the house. "We are not much altered in our ways, are we, my Lord?" he said as he moved a bottle of whiskey that stood on the sideboard. "Shall I offer you lunch?"

"No, thank you, Father Marty; — nothing, thank you." Then he made a gasp and began. The bad hour had arrived, and it must be endured. "I have come back, as you see, Father Marty. That was a matter of course."

"Well, yes, my Lord. As things have gone it

was a matter of course."

"I am here. I came as soon as it was possible that I should come. Of course it was necessary that I should remain at home for some days after what has occurred at Scroope."

"No doubt; — no doubt. But you will not be angry with me for saying that after what has occurred here, your presence has been most anxiously expected. However here you are, and all may yet be well. As God's minister I ought perhaps to upbraid. But I am not given to much upbraiding, and I love that dear and innocent young face too well to desire anything now but that the owner of it should receive at your hands that which is due to her before God and man."

He perceived that the priest knew it all. But how could he wonder at this when that which ought to have been her secret and his had become known even to Lady Mary Quin? And he understood well what the priest meant when he spoke of that which was due to Kate O'Hara before God and man; and he could perceive, or thought that he perceived, that the priest did not doubt of the coming marriage, now that he, the victim, was again back in the west of Ireland. And was he not the victim of a scheme? Had he not been allured on to make promises to the girl which he would not have made had the truth been told him as to her father? He would not even in his thoughts accuse Kate, — his Kate, — of being a participator in these schemes. But Mrs. O'Hara and the priest had certainly intrigued against him. He must remember that. In the terrible task which he was now compelled to begin he must build his defence chiefly upon that. Yes; he must begin his work, now, upon the instant. With all his golden prospects, — with all his golden honours already in his possession, — he could wish himself dead rather than begin it. But he could not die and have done it. "Father. Marty," he said, "I cannot make Miss O'Hara Countess of Scroope."

"Not make her Countess of Scroope! What will you make her then?"

"As to that, I am here to discuss it with you."

"What is it you main, sir? Afther you have had your will of her, and polluted her sweet innocence, you will not make her your wife! You cannot look me in the face, Mr. Neville, and tell me that."

There the priest was right. The young Earl could not look him in the face as he stammered out his explanation and proposal. The burly, strong old man stood perfectly still and silent as he, with hesitating and ill-arranged words, tried to gloze over and make endurable his past conduct and intentions as to the future. He still held some confused idea as to a form of marriage which should for all his life bind him to the woman, but which should give her no claim to the title, and her child no claim either to the title or the property. "You should have told me of this Captain O'Hara," he said, as with many

259

half-formed sentences he completed his suggestions.

"And it's on me you are throwing the blame?"

"You should have told me, Father Marty."

"By the great God above me, I did not believe that a man could be such a villain! As I look for glory I did not think it possible! I should have tould you! Neither did I nor did Mistress O'Hara know or believe that the man was alive. And what has the man to do with it? Is she vile because he has been guilty? Is she other than you knew her to be when you first took her to your bosom, because of his sin?"

"It does make a difference, Mr. Marty."

"Afther what you have done it can make no difference. When you swore to her that she should be your wife, and conquered her by so swearing, was there any clause in your contract that you were not to be bound if you found aught displaising to you in her parentage?"

"I ought to have known it all."

"You knew all that she knew; — all that I knew. You knew all that her mother knew. No, Lord Scroope. It cannot be that you should be so unutterably a villain. You are your own masther. Unsay what you have said to me, and her ears shall never be wounded or her heart broken by a hint of it."

"I cannot make her Countess of Scroope. You are a priest, and can use what words you please to me; — but I cannot make her Countess of Scroope."

"Faith, — and there will be more than words used, my young lord. As to your plot of a counterfeit marriage, —"

"I said nothing of a counterfeit marriage."

"What was it you said, then? I say you did. You proposed to me, — to me a priest of God's altar, — a false counterfeit marriage, so that those two poor women, who you are afraid to face, might be cajoled and chaited and ruined."

"I am going to face them instantly."

"Then must your heart be made of very stone. Shall I tell you the consequences?" Then the priest paused awhile, and the young man, bursting into tears, hid his face against the wall. "I will tell you the consequences, Lord Scroope. They will die. The shame and sorrow which you have brought on them, will bring them to their graves, — and so there will be an end of their throubles upon earth. But while I live there shall be no rest for the sole of your foot. I am ould, and may soon be below the sod, but I will lave it as a legacy behind me that your iniquity shall be proclaimed and made known in high places. While I live I will follow you, and when I am gone there shall be another to take the work. My curse shall rest on you, — the curse of a man of God, and you shall be accursed. Now, if it suits you, you can go up to them at Ardkill and tell them your story. She is waiting to receive her lover. You can go to her, and stab her to the heart at once. Go, sir! Unless you can change all this and alter your heart even as you hear my words,

261

you are unfit to find shelter beneath my roof."

Having so spoken, waiting to see the effect of his indignation, the priest went out, and got upon his horse, and went away upon his journey. The young lord knew that he had been insulted, was aware that words had been said to him so severe that one man, in his rank of life, rarely utters them to another; and he had stood the while with his face turned to the wall speechless and sobbing! The priest had gone, telling him to leave the house because his presence disgraced it; and he had made no answer. Yet he was the Earl of Scroope, — the thirteenth Earl of Scroope, — a man in his own country full of honours. Why had he come there to be called a villain? And why was the world so hard upon him that on hearing himself so called he could only weep like a girl? Had he done worse than other men? Was he not willing to make any retribution for his fault, — except by doing that which he had been taught to think would be a greater fault? As he left the house he tried to harden his heart against Kate O'Hara. The priest had lied to him about her father. They must have known that the man was alive. They had caught him among them, and the priest's anger was a part of the net with which they had intended to surround him. The stake for which they had played had been very great. To be Countess of Scroope was indeed a chance worth some risk. Then, as he breasted the hill up towards the burial ground, he tried to strengthen his courage by realizing the magnitude of his own position. He bade himself remember that he was among people who were his inferiors in rank, education, wealth, manners, religion and nationality. He had committed an error. Of course he had been in fault. Did he wish to escape the consequences of his own misdoing? Was not his presence there so soon after the assumption of his family honours sufficient evidence of his generous admission of the claims to which he was subject? Had he not offered to sacrifice himself as no other man would have done? But they were still playing for the high stakes. They were determined that the girl should be Countess of Scroope. He was determined that she should not be Countess of Scroope. He was still willing to sacrifice himself, but his family honours he would not pollute.

And then as he made his way past the burial ground and on towards the cliff there crept over him a feeling as to the girl very different from that reverential love which he had bestowed upon her when she was still pure. He remembered the poorness of her raiment, the meekness of her language, the small range of her ideas. The sweet soft coaxing loving smile, which had once been so dear to him, was infantine and ignoble. She was a plaything for an idle hour, not a woman to be taken out into the world with the high name of Countess of Scroope.

All this was the antagonism in his own heart against the indignant words which the priest had

spoken to him. For a moment he was so overcome that he had burst into tears. But not on
that account would he be beaten away from his
decision. The priest had called him a villain and
had threatened and cursed him! As to the vil-
lainy he had already made up his mind which
way his duty lay. For the threats it did not
become him to count them as anything. The
curses were the result of the man's barbarous
religion. He remembered that he was the Earl of
Scroope, and so remembering summoned up his
courage as he walked on to the cottage.

CHAPTER X.
AT ARDKILL.

Sharp eyes had watched for the young lord's approach. As he came near to the cottage the door was opened and Kate O'Hara rushed out to meet him. Though his mind was turned against her, — was turned against her as hard and fast as all his false reasonings had been able to make it, — he could not but accord to her the reception of a lover. She was in his arms and he could not but press her close to his bosom. Her face was held up to his, and of course he covered it with kisses. She murmured to him sweet warm words of passionate love, and he could not but answer with endearing names. "I am your own, — am I not?" she said as she still clung to him. "All my own," he whispered as he tightened his arm round her waist.

Then he asked after Mrs. O'Hara. "Yes; mother is there. She will be almost as glad to see you as I am. Nobody can be quite so glad. Oh Fred, — my darling Fred, — am I still to call you Fred?"

"What else, my pet?"

"I was thinking whether I would call you — my Lord."

"For heaven's sake do not."

"No. You shall be Fred, — my Fred; Fred to me, though all the world besides may call you grand names." Then again she held up her face to him and pressed the hand that was round her waist closer to her girdle. To have him once more with her, — this was to taste all the joys of heaven while she was still on earth.

They entered the sitting-room together and met Mrs. O'Hara close to the door. "My Lord," she said, "you are very welcome back to us. Indeed we need you much. I will not upbraid you as you come to make atonement for your fault. If you will let me I will love you as a son." As she spoke she held his right hand in both of hers, and then she lifted up her face and kissed his cheek.

He could not stay her words, nor could he refuse the kiss. And yet to him the kiss was as the kiss of Judas, and the words were false words, plotted words, pre-arranged, so that after hearing them there should be no escape for him. But he would escape. He resolved again, even then, that he would escape; but he could not answer her words at the moment. Though Mrs. O'Hara held him by the hand, Kate still hung to his other arm. He could not thrust her away from him. She still clung to him when he released his right hand, and almost lay upon his breast when he seated himself on the sofa. She looked into his eyes for tenderness, and he could not refrain himself from bestowing upon her the happiness.

"Oh, mother," she said, "he is so brown; — but he is handsomer than ever." But though he smiled on her, giving back into her eyes her own soft look of love, yet he must tell his tale.

He was still minded that she should have all but the one thing, — all if she would take it. She should not be Countess of Scroope; but in any other respect he would pay what penalty might be required for his transgression. But in what words should he explain this to those two women? Mrs. O'Hara had called him by his title and had claimed him as her son. No doubt she had all the right to do so which promises made by himself could give her. He had sworn that he would marry the girl, and in point of time had only limited his promise by the old Earl's life. The old Earl was dead, and he stood pledged to the immediate performance of his vow, — doubly pledged if he were at all solicitous for the honour of his future bride. But in spite of all promises she should never be Countess of Scroope!

Some tinkling false-tongued phrase as to lover's oaths had once passed across his memory and had then sufficed to give him a grain of comfort. There was no comfort to be found in it now. He began to tell himself, in spite of his manhood, that it might have been better for him and for them that he should have broken this matter to them by a well-chosen messenger. But it was too late for that now. He had faced the priest and had escaped from him with the degradation of a few tears. Now he was in the presence of the lioness and her young. The lioness had claimed him as a denizen of the forest; and, would he yield to her, she no doubt would be very tender to him. But, as he was resolved not to yield, he began to find that he had been wrong to enter her den. As he looked at her, knowing that she was at this moment softened by false hopes, he could nevertheless see in her eye the wrath of the wild animal. How was he to begin to make his purpose known to them.

"And now you must tell us everything," said Kate, still encircled by his arm.

"What must I tell you?"

"You will give up the regiment at once?"

"I have done so already."

"But you must not give up Ardkill; — must he, mother?"

"He may give it up when he takes you from it, Kate."

"But he will take you too, mother?"

The lioness at any rate wanted nothing for herself. "No, love. I shall remain here among my rocks, and shall be happy if I hear that you are happy."

"But you won't part us altogether, — will you, Fred?"

"No, love."

"I knew he wouldn't. And mother may come to your grand house and creep into some pretty little corner there, where I can go and visit her, and tell her that she shall always be my own,

own, own darling mother."

He felt that he must put a stop to this in some way, though the doing of it would be very dreadful. Indeed in the doing of it the whole of his task would consist. But still he shirked it, and used his wit in contriving an answer which might still deceive without being false in words. "I think," said he, "that I shall never live at any grand house, as you call it."

"Not live at Scroope?" asked Mrs. O'Hara.

"I think not. It will hardly suit me."

"I shall not regret it," said Kate. "I care nothing for a grand house. I should only be afraid of it. I know it is dark and sombre, for you have said so. Oh, Fred, any place will be Paradise to me, if I am there with you."

He felt that every moment of existence so continued was a renewed lie. She was lying in his arms, in her mother's presence, almost as his acknowledged wife. And she was speaking of her future home as being certainly his also. But what could he do? How could he begin to tell the truth? His home should be her home, if she would come to him, — not as his wife. That idea of some half-valid morganatic marriage had again been dissipated by the rough reproaches of the priest, and could only be used as a prelude to his viler proposal. And, though he loved the girl after his fashion, he desired to wound her by no such vile proposal. He did not wish to live a life of sin, if such life might be avoided. If he made his proposal, it would be but for her sake;

or rather that he might show her that he did not wish to cast her aside. It was by asserting to himself that for her sake he would relinquish his own rank, were that possible, that he attempted to relieve his own conscience. But, in the mean time, she was in his arms talking about their joint future home! "Where do you think of living?" asked Mrs. O'Hara in a tone which shewed plainly the anxiety with which she asked the question.

"Probably abroad," he said.

"But mother may go with us?" The girl felt that the tension of his arm was relaxed, and she knew that all was not well with him. And if there was ought amiss with him, how much more must it be amiss with her? "What is it, Fred?" she said. "There is some secret. Will you not tell it to me?" Then she whispered into his ear words intended for him alone, though her mother heard them. "If there be a secret you should tell it me now. Think how it is with me. Your words are life and death to me now." He still held her with loosened arms but did not answer her. He sat, looking out into the middle of the room with fixed eyes, and he felt that drops of perspiration were on his brow. And he knew that the other woman was glaring at him with the eyes of an injured lioness, though he did not dare to turn his own to her face. "Fred, tell me; tell me." And Kate rose up, with her knees upon the sofa, bending over him, gazing into his countenance and imploring him.

"There must be disappointment," he said; and he did not know the sound of his own voice.

"What disappointment? Speak to me. What disappointment?"

"Disappointment!" shrieked the mother. "How disappointment? There shall be no disappointment." Rising from her chair, she hurried across the room, and took her girl from his arms. "Lord Scroope, tell us what you mean. I say there shall be no disappointment. Sit away from him, Kate, till he has told us what it is." Then they heard the sound of a horse's foot passing close to the window, and they all knew that it was the priest. "There is Father Marty," said Mrs. O'Hara. "He shall make you tell it."

"I have already told him." Lord Scroope as he said this rose and moved towards the door; but he himself was almost unconscious of the movement. Some idea probably crossed his mind that he would meet the priest, but Mrs. O'Hara thought that he intended to escape from them.

She rushed between him and the door and held him with both her hands. "No; no; you do not leave us in that way, though you were twice an Earl."

"I am not thinking of leaving you."

"Mother, you shall not hurt him; you shall not insult him," said the girl. "He does not mean to harm me. He is my own, and no one shall touch him."

"Certainly I will not harm you. Here is Father Marty. Mrs. O'Hara you had better be tranquil.

You should remember that you have heard nothing yet of what I would say to you."

"Whose fault is that? Why do you not speak? Father Marty, what does he mean when he tells my girl that there must be disappointment for her? Does he dare to tell me that he hesitates to make her his wife?"

The priest took the mother by the hand and placed her on the chair in which she usually sat. Then, almost without a word, he led Kate from the room to her own chamber, and bade her wait a minute till he should come back to her. Then he returned to the sitting-room and at once addressed himself to Lord Scroope. "Have you dared," he said, "to tell them what you hardly dared to tell to me?"

"He has dared to tell us nothing," said Mrs. O'Hara.

"I do not wonder at it. I do not think that any man could say to her that which he told me that he would do."

"Mrs. O'Hara," said the young lord, with some return of courage now that the girl had left them, "that which I told Mr. Marty this morning, I will now tell to you. For your daughter I will do anything that you and she and he may wish, — but one thing. I cannot make her Countess of Scroope."

"You must make her your wife," said the woman, shouting at him.

"I will do so to-morrow if a way can be found by which she shall not become Countess of

Scroope."

"That is, he will marry her without making her his wife," said the priest. "He will jump over a broomstick with her and will ask me to help him, — so that your feelings and hers may be spared for a week or so. Mrs. O'Hara, he is a villain, — a vile, heartless, cowardly reprobate, so low in the scale of humanity that I degrade myself by spaking to him. He calls himself an English peer! Peer to what? Certainly to no one worthy to be called a man!" So speaking, the priest addressed himself to Mrs. O'Hara, but as he spoke his eyes were fixed full on the face of the young lord.

"I will have his heart out of his body," exclaimed Mrs. O'Hara.

"Heart; — he has no heart. You may touch his pocket; — or his pride, what he calls his pride, a damnable devilish inhuman vanity; or his name, — that bugbear of a title by which he trusts to cover his baseness; or his skin, for he is a coward. Do you see his cheek now? But as for his heart, — you cannot get at that."

"I will get at his life," said the woman.

"Mr. Marty, you allow yourself a liberty of speech which even your priesthood will not warrant."

"Lay a hand upon me if you can. There is not blood enough about you to do it. Were it not that the poor child has been wake and too trusting, I would bid her spit on you rather than take you for her husband." Then he paused, but only for a moment. "Sir, you must marry her, and there must be an end of it. In no other way can you be allowed to live."

"Would you murder me?"

"I would crush you like an insect beneath my nail. Murder you! Have you thought what murder is; — that there are more ways of murder than one? Have you thought of the life of that young girl who now bears in her womb the fruit of your body? Would you murder her, — because she loved you, and trusted you, and gave you all simply because you asked her; and then think of your own life? As the God of Heaven is above me, and sees me now, and the Saviour in whose blood I trust, I would lay down my life this instant, if I could save her from your heartlessness." So saying he too turned away his face and wept like a child.

After this the priest was gentler in his manner to the young man, and it almost seemed as though the Earl was driven from his decision. He ceased, at any rate, to assert that Kate should never be Countess of Scroope, and allowed both the mother and Father Marty to fall into a state of doubt as to what his last resolve might be. It was decided that he should go down to Ennistimon and sleep upon it. On the morrow he would come up again, and in the meantime he would see Father Marty at the inn. There were many prayers addressed to him both by the mother and the priest, and such arguments used that he had been almost shaken. "But you will come to-morrow?" said the mother, looking at the priest as she spoke.

"I will certainly come to-morrow."

"No doubt he will come to-morrow," said Father Marty, — who intended to imply that if Lord Scroope escaped out of Ennistimon without his knowledge, he would be very much surprised.

"Shall I not say a word to Kate?" the Earl asked as he was going.

"Not till you are prepared to tell her that she shall be your wife," said the priest.

But this was a matter as to which Kate herself had a word to say. When they were in the passage she came out from her room, and again rushed into her lover's arms. "Oh, Fred, let me told, — let me told. I will go with you anywhere if you will take me."

"He is to come up to-morrow, Kate," said her mother.

"He will be here early to-morrow, and everything shall be settled then," said the priest, trying to assume a happy and contented tone.

"Dearest Kate, I will be here by noon," said Lord Scroope, returning the girl's caresses.

"And you will not desert me?"

"No, darling, no." And then he went, leaving the priest behind him at the cottage.

Father Marty was to be with him at the inn by eight, and then the whole matter must be again discussed. He felt that he had been very weak, that he had made no use, — almost no use at all, — of the damning fact of the Captain's existence. He had allowed the priest to talk him down in every argument, and had been actually awed by the girl's mother, and yet he was determined that he would not yield. He felt more strongly than ever, now that he had again seen Kate O'Hara, that it would not be right that such a one as she should be made Countess of Scroope. Not only would she disgrace the place, but she would be unhappy in it, and would shame him. After all the promises that he had made he could not, and he would not, take her to Scroope as his wife. How could she hold up her head before such women as Sophie Mellerby and others like her? It would be known by all his friends that he had been taken in and swindled by low people in the County Clare, and he would be regarded by all around him as one who had absolutely ruined himself. He had positively resolved that she should not be Countess of Scroope, and to that resolution he would adhere. The foul-mouthed priest had called him a coward, but he would be no coward. The mother had said that she would have his life. If there were danger in that respect he must encounter it. As he returned to Ennistimon he again determined that Kate O'Hara should never become Countess of Scroope.

For three hours Father Marty remained with him that night, but did not shake him. He had now become accustomed to the priest's wrath and could endure it. And he thought also that he could now endure the mother. The tears of the girl and her reproaches he still did fear.

"I will do anything that you can dictate short of that," he said again to Father Marty.

"Anything but the one thing that you have sworn to do?"

"Anything but the one thing that I have sworn not to do." For he had told the priest of the promises he had made both to his uncle and to his uncle's widow.

"Then," said the priest, as he crammed his hat on his head, and shook the dust off his feet, "if I were you I would not go to Ardkill to-morrow if I valued my life." Nevertheless Father Marty slept at Ennistimon that night, and was prepared to bar the way if any attempt at escape were made.

CHAPTER XI.
ON THE CLIFFS.

No attempt at escape was made. The Earl breakfasted by himself at about nine, and then lighting a cigar, roamed about for a while round the Inn, thinking of the work that was now before him. He saw nothing of Father Marty though he knew that the priest was still in Ennistimon. And he felt that he was watched. They might have saved themselves that trouble, for he certainly had no intention of breaking his word to them. So he told himself, thinking as he did so, that people such as these could not understand that an Earl of Scroope would not be untrue to his word. And yet since he had been back in County Clare he had almost regretted that he had not broken his faith to them and remained in England. At half-past ten he started on a car, having promised to be at the cottage at noon, and he told his servant that he should certainly leave Ennistimon that day at three. The horse and gig were to be ready for him exactly at that hour.

On this occasion he did not go through Liscannor, but took the other road to the burial ground. There he left his car and slowly walked along the cliffs till he came to the path leading down from them to the cottage. In doing this he went somewhat out of his way, but he had time on his hands and he did not desire to be at the cottage before the hour he had named. It was a hot midsummer day, and there seemed to be hardly a ripple on the waves. The tide was full in, and he sat for a while looking down upon the blue waters. What an ass had he made himself, coming thither in quest of adventures! He began to see now the meaning of such idleness of purpose as that to which he had looked for pleasure and excitement. Even the ocean itself and the very rocks had lost their charm for him. It was all one blaze of blue light, the sky above and the water below, in which there was neither beauty nor variety. How poor had been the life he had chosen! He had spent hour after hour in a comfortless dirty boat, in company with a wretched ignorant creature, in order that he might shoot a few birds and possibly a seal. All the world had been open to him, and yet how miserable had been his ambition! And now he could see no way out of the ruin he had brought upon himself.

When the time had come he rose from his seat and took the path down to the cottage. At the corner of the little patch of garden ground attached to it he met Mrs. O'Hara. Her hat was on her head, and a light shawl was on her shoulders as though she had prepared herself for walking. He immediately asked after Kate. She told him that Kate was within and should see him presently. Would it not be better that they two should go up on the cliffs together, and then say what might be necessary for the mutual understanding of their purposes? "There should be no talking of all this before Kate," said Mrs. O'Hara.

"That is true."

"You can imagine what she must feel if she is told to doubt. Lord Scroope, will you not say at once that there shall be no doubt? You must not ruin my child in return for her love!"

"If there must be ruin I would sooner bear it myself," said he. And then they walked on without further speech till they had reached a point somewhat to the right, and higher than that on which he had sat before. It had ever been a favourite spot with her, and he had often sat there between the mother and daughter. It was almost the summit of the cliff, but there was yet a higher pitch which screened it from the north, so that the force of the wind was broken. The fall from it was almost precipitous to the ocean, so that the face of the rocks immediately below was not in view; but there was a curve here in the line of the shore, and a little bay in the coast, which exposed to view the whole side of the op-posite cliff, so that the varying colours of the rocks might be seen. The two ladies had made a seat upon the turf, by moving the loose stones and levelling the earth around, so that they could sit securely on the very edge. Many many hours had Mrs. O'Hara passed upon the spot, both summer and winter, watching the sunset in the west, and listening to the screams of the birds. "There are no gulls now," she said as she seated herself, — as though for a moment she had forgotten the great subject which filled her mind.

"No; — they never show themselves in weather like this. They only come when the wind blows. I wonder where they go when the sun shines."

"They are just the opposite to men and women who only come around you in fine weather. How hot it is!" and she threw her shawl back from her shoulders.

"Yes, indeed. I walked up from the burial ground and I found that it was very hot. Have you seen Father Marty this morning?"

"No. Have you?" she asked the question turning upon him very shortly.

"Not to-day. He was with me till late last night."

"Well." He did not answer her. He had nothing to say to her. In fact everything had been said yesterday. If she had questions to ask he would answer them. "What did you settle last night? When he went from me an hour after you were gone, he said that it was impossible that you should mean to destroy her."

"God forbid that I should destroy her."

"He said that, — that you were afraid of her father."

"I am."

"And of me."

"No; — not of you, Mrs. O'Hara."

"Listen to me. He said that such a one as you cannot endure the presence of an uneducated and ill-mannered mother-in-law. Do not interrupt me, Lord Scroope. If you will marry her, my girl shall never see my face again; and I will cling to that man and will not leave him for a moment, so that he shall never put his foot near your door. Our name shall never be spoken in your hearing. She shall never even write to me if you think it better that we shall be so separated."

"It is not that," he said.

"What is it, then?"

"Oh, Mrs. O'Hara, you do not understand. You, — you I could love dearly."

"I would have you keep all your love for her."

"I do love her. She is good enough for me. She is too good; and so are you. It is for the family, and not for myself."

"How will she harm the family?"

"I swore to my uncle that I would not make her Countess of Scroope."

"And have you not sworn to her again and again that she should be your wife? Do you think that she would have done for you what she has done, had you not so sworn? Lord Scroope, I cannot think that you really mean it." She put both her hands softly upon his arm and looked up to him imploring his mercy.

He got up from his seat and roamed along the cliff, and she followed him, still imploring. Her tones were soft, and her words were the words of a suppliant. Would he not relent and save her child from wretchedness, from ruin and from death. "I will keep her with me till I die," he said.

"But not as your wife?"

"She shall have all attention from me, — everything that a woman's heart can desire. You two shall be never separated."

"But not as your wife?"

"I will live where she and you may please. She shall want nothing that my wife would possess."

"But not as your wife?"

"Not as Countess of Scroope."

"You would have her as your mistress, then?" As she asked this question the tone of her voice was altogether altered, and the threatening lion-look had returned to her eyes. They were now near the seat, confronted to each other; and the fury of her bosom, which for a while had been dominated by the tenderness of the love for her daughter, was again raging within her. Was it possible that he should be able to treat them thus, — that he should break his word and go from them scathless, happy, joyous, with all the delights of the world before him, leaving them crushed into dust beneath his feet. She had been called upon from her youth upwards to bear injustice, — but of all injustice surely this would be the worst. "As your mistress," she repeated, — "and I her mother, am to stand by and see it, and know that my girl is dishonoured! Would your mother have borne that for your sister? How would it be if your sister were as that girl is now?"

"I have no sister."

"And therefore you are thus hard-hearted. She shall never be your harlot; — never. I would myself sooner take from her the life I gave her. You have destroyed her, but she shall never be a thing so low as that."

"I will marry her, — in a foreign land."

"And why not here? She is as good as you. Why should she not bear the name you are so proud of dinning into our ears? Why should she not be a Countess? Has she ever disgraced herself? If she is disgraced in your eyes you must be a Devil."

"It is not that," he said hoarsely.

"What is it? What has she done that she should be thus punished? Tell me, man, that she shall be your lawful wife." As she said this she caught him roughly by the collar of his coat and shook him with her arm.

"It cannot be so," said the Earl Of Scroope.

"It cannot be so! But I say it shall, — or, — or — ! What are you, that she should be in your hands like this? Say that she shall be your wife, or you shall never live to speak to another woman." The peril of his position on the top of the cliff had not occurred to him; — nor did it occur to him now. He had been there so often that the place gave him no sense of danger. Nor had that peril, — as it was thought afterwards by those who most closely made inquiry on the matter, — ever occurred to her. She had not brought him there that she might frighten him with that danger, or that she might avenge herself by the power which it gave her. But now the idea flashed across her maddened mind. "Miscreant," she said. And she bore him back to the very edge of the precipice.

"You'll have me over the cliff," he exclaimed hardly even yet putting out his strength against her.

"And so I will, by the help of God. Now think of her! Now think of her!" And as she spoke she pressed him backwards towards his fall. He had power enough to bend his knee, and to crouch beneath her grasp on to the loose crumbling soil of the margin of the rocks. He still held her by her cuff and it seemed for a moment as though she must go with him. But, on a sudden, she spurned him with her foot on the breast, the rag of cloth parted in his hand, and the poor wretch tumbled forth alone into eternity.

That was the end of Frederic Neville, Earl of Scroope, and the end, too, of all that poor girl's hopes in this world. When you stretch yourself on the edge of those cliffs and look down over the abyss on the sea below it seems as though the rocks were so absolutely perpendicular, that a stone dropped with an extended hand would fall amidst the waves. But in such measurement the eye deceives itself, for the rocks in truth slant down; and the young man, as he fell, struck them again and again; and at last it was a broken mangled corpse that reached the blue waters below.

Her Kate was at last avenged. The woman stood there in her solitude for some minutes thinking of the thing she had done. The man had injured her, — sorely, — and she had punished him. He had richly deserved the death which he had received from her hands. In these minutes, as regarded him, there was no remorse. But how should she tell the news to her child? The blow which had thrust him over would, too probably, destroy other life than his. Would it not be better that her girl should so die? What could prolonged life give her that would be worth her having? As for herself, — in these first moments of her awe she took no thought of her own danger. It did not occur to her that she might tell how the man had ventured too near the edge and had fallen by mischance. As regarded herself she was proud of the thing she had accomplished; but how should she tell her child that it was done?

She slowly took the path, not to the cottage, but down towards the burial ground and Liscannor, passing the car which was waiting in vain for the young lord. On she walked with rapid step, indifferent to the heat, still proud of what she had done, — raging with a maddened pride. How little had they two asked of the world! And then this man had come to them and robbed them of all that little, had spoiled them ruthlessly, cheating them with lies, and then excusing himself by the grandeur of his blood! During that walk it was that she first repeated to herself the words that were ever afterwards on her tongue; An Eye for an Eye. Was not that justice? And, had she not taken the eye herself, would any Court in the world have given it to her? Yes; — an eye for an eye! Death in return for ruin! One destruction for another! The punishment had been just. An eye for an eye! Let the Courts of the world now say what they pleased, they could not return to his earldom the man who had plundered and spoiled her child. He had sworn that he would not make her Kate Countess of Scroope! Nor should he make any other woman a Countess!

Rapidly she went down by the burying ground, and into the priest's house. Father Marty was there, and she stalked at once into his presence. "Ha; — Mrs. O'Hara! And where is Lord Scroope?"

"There," she said, pointing out towards the ocean. "Under the rocks!"

"He has fallen!"

"I thrust him down with my hands and with my feet." As she said this, she used her hand and her foot as though she were now using her strength to push the man over the edge. "Yes, I thrust him down, and he fell splashing into the waves. I heard it as his body struck the water. He will shoot no more of the sea-gulls now."

"You do not mean that you have murdered him?"

"You may call it murder if you please, Father Marty. An eye for an eye, Father Marty! It is justice, and I have done it. An Eye for an Eye!"

Chapter XII.
Conclusion.

The story of the poor mad woman who still proclaims in her seclusion the justice of the deed which she did, has now been told. It may perhaps be well to collect the scattered ends of the threads of the tale for the benefit of readers who desire to know the whole of a history.

Mrs. O'Hara never returned to the cottage on the cliffs after the perpetration of the deed. On the unhappy priest devolved the duty of doing whatever must be done. The police at the neighbouring barracks were told that the young lord had perished by a fall from the cliffs, and by them search was made for the body. No real attempt was set on foot to screen the woman who had done the deed by any concealment of the facts. She herself was not alive to the necessity of making any such attempt. "An eye for an eye!" she said to the head-constable when the man interrogated her. It soon became known to all Liscannor, to Ennistimon, to the ladies at Castle Quin, and to all the barony of Corcomroe that Mrs. O'Hara had thrust the Earl of Scroope over the cliffs of Moher, and that she was now detained at the house of Father Marty in the custody of a policeman. Before the day was over it was declared also that she was mad, — and that her daughter was dying.

The deed which the woman had done and the death of the young lord were both terrible to Father Marty; but there was a duty thrown upon him more awful to his mind even than these. Kate O'Hara, when her mother appeared at the priest's house, had been alone at the cottage. By degrees Father Marty learned from the wretched woman something of the circumstances of that morning's work. Kate had not seen her lover that day, but had been left in the cottage while her mother went out to meet the man, and if possible to persuade him to do her child justice. The priest understood that she would be waiting for them, — or more probably searching for them on the cliffs. He got upon his horse and rode up the hill with a heavy heart. What should he tell her; and how should he tell it?

Before he reached the cottage she came running down the hillside to him. "Father Marty, where is mother? Where is Mr. Neville? You know. I see that you know. Where are they?" He got off his horse and put his arm round her body and seated her beside himself on the rising bank by the wayside. "Why don't you speak?" she said.

"I cannot speak," he murmured. "I cannot tell you."

"Is he — dead?" He only buried his face in his hands. "She has killed him! Mother — mother!"

290

Then, with one loud long wailing shriek, she fell upon the ground.

Not for a month after that did she know anything of what happened around her. But yet it seemed that during that time her mind had not been altogether vacant, for when she awoke to self-consciousness, she knew at least that her lover was dead. She had been taken into Ennistimon and there, under the priest's care, had been tended with infinite solicitude; but almost with a hope on his part that nature might give way and that she might die. Overwhelmed as she was with sorrows past and to come would it not be better for her that she should go hence and be no more seen? But as Death cannot be barred from the door when he knocks at it, so neither can he be made to come as a guest when summoned. She still lived, though life had so little to offer to her.

But Mrs. O'Hara never saw her child again. With passionate entreaties she begged of the police that her girl might be brought to her, that she might be allowed if it were only to see her face or to touch her hand. Her entreaties to the priest, who was constant in his attendance upon her in the prison to which she was removed from his house, were piteous, — almost heartbreaking. But the poor girl, though she was meek, silent, and almost apathetic in her tranquillity, could not even bear the mention of her mother's name. Her mother had destroyed the father of the child that was to be born to her, her lover,

291

her hero, her god; and in her remembrance of the man who had betrayed her, she learned to execrate the mother who had sacrificed everything, — her very reason, — in avenging the wrongs of her child!

Mrs. O'Hara was taken away from the priest's house to the County Gaol, but was then in a condition of acknowledged insanity. That she had committed the murder no one who heard the story doubted, but of her guilt there was no evidence whatever beyond the random confession of a maniac. No detailed confession was ever made by her. "An eye for an eye," she would say when interrogated, — "Is not that justice? A tooth for a tooth!" Though she was for a while detained in prison it was impossible to prosecute her, — even with a view to an acquittal on the ground of insanity; and while the question was under discussion among the lawyers, provision for her care and maintenance came from another source.

As also it did for the poor girl. For a while everything was done for her under the care of Father Marty; — but there was another Earl of Scroope in the world, and as soon as the story was known to him and the circumstances had been made clear, he came forward to offer on behalf of the family whatever assistance might now avail them anything. As months rolled on the time of Kate O'Hara's further probation came, but Fate spared her the burden and despair of a living infant. It was at last thought better that she should go to her father and live in France with him, reprobate though the man was. The priest offered to find a home for her in his own house at Liscannor; but, as he said himself, he was an old man, and one who when he went would leave no home behind him. And then it was felt that the close vicinity of the spot on which her lover had perished would produce a continued melancholy that might crush her spirits utterly. Captain O'Hara therefore was desired to come and fetch his child, — and he did so, with many protestations of virtue for the future. If actual pecuniary comfort can conduce to virtue in such a man, a chance was given him. The Earl of Scroope was only too liberal in the settlement he made. But the settlement was on the daughter and not on the father; and it is possible therefore that some gentle restraint may have served to keep him out of the deep abysses of wickedness.

The effects of the tragedy on the coast of Clare spread beyond Ireland, and drove another woman to the verge of insanity. When the Countess of Scroope heard the story, she shut herself up at Scroope and would see no one but her own servants. When the succeeding Earl came to the house which was now his own, she refused to admit him into her presence, and declined even a renewed visit from Miss Mellerby who at that time had returned to her father's roof. At last the clergyman of Scroope prevailed, and to him she unburdened her soul,

— acknowledging, with an energy that went perhaps beyond the truth, the sin of her own conduct in producing the catastrophe which had occurred. "I knew that he had wronged her, and yet I bade him not to make her his wife." That was the gist of her confession and she declared that the young man's blood would be on her hands till she died. A small cottage was prepared for her on the estate, and there she lived in absolute seclusion till death relieved her from her sorrows.

And she lived not only in seclusion, but in solitude almost to her death. It was not till four years after the occurrences which have been here related that John fourteenth Earl of Scroope brought a bride home to Scroope Manor. The reader need hardly be told that that bride was Sophie Mellerby. When the young Countess came to live at the Manor the old Countess admitted her visits and at last found some consolation in her friend's company. But it lasted not long, and then she was taken away and buried beside her lord in the chancel of the parish church.

When it was at last decided that the law should not interfere at all as to the personal custody of the poor maniac who had sacrificed everything to avenge her daughter, the Earl of Scroope selected for her comfort the asylum in which she still continues to justify from morning to night, and, alas, often all the night long, the terrible deed of which she is ever thinking. "An eye for an eye," she says to the woman who watches her.

"Oh, yes, ma'am; certainly."

"An eye for an eye, and a tooth for a tooth! Is it not so? An eye for an eye!"

The employees of Thorndike Press hope you have enjoyed this Large Print book. All our Thorndike, Wheeler, and Kennebec Large Print titles are designed for easy reading, and all our books are made to last. Other Thorndike Press Large Print books are available at your library, through selected bookstores, or directly from us.

For information about titles, please call:
  (800) 223-1244

or visit our Web site at:
  http://gale.cengage.com/thorndike

To share your comments, please write:
  Publisher
  Thorndike Press
  295 Kennedy Memorial Drive
  Waterville, ME 04901